£1.50

From

The Women's Press Ltd
34 Great Sutton Street, London EC1V 0DX

CW00952171

URSULE MOLINARO

Positions with White Roses

The Women's Press

First published in Great Britain by
The Women's Press Limited 1988
A member of the Namara Group
34 Great Sutton Street, London EC1V 0DX

First published in the United States by McPherson & Company,
Box 638, New Paltz, NY 12561, 1983

British Library Cataloguing in Publication Data available

The author gratefully acknowledges receipt of a grant from Creative Artists
Program Services Inc. which assisted the writing of this novel.

The characters are composites of true-life models. The landscapes are pure fiction.

Printed and bound in Great Britain by
Cox & Wyman Ltd, Reading

A Novel in the Form of a Cross

For Eunie
Tina
Sandy (& Sally)
Honor & India
Helen M.
Mary N.
Cindy, my painlessly acquired daughter
& the many unsuspected twins
that came out of the woodwork
while this novel was incubating

The visiting daughter sits
between them, at one of
the long sides of the long,
highly polished grey mar-
ble dining table.
Which they brought with
them when they left Flor-
ence. Early enough to
leave with all their furniture. Everything in their
house is cedar, &
rosewood, & marble.
Everything is at least 150
years old.

They left Italy because they were Jews. Which most of
their friends & neighbors hadn't known until they left.
The families they came from had deep Italian roots.
With a memory of persecution on the father's side: a
Bologna ancestor had been burned alive for digging up
corpses to study diseases, & one of his mother's great-
grandaunts had been drowned in the Arno for deliver-
ing a noblewoman of twins.
It was at the father's insistence that they left before
they became refugees:

A 28-year-old physician, a neo-dottore, leaving the
recently inherited family practice in Florence to
become an embalmer, in San Francisco.
_____Which he chose for the name: an outpost of
Assisi, a bridgehead. Poring over maps of their future
exile, pointing to consoling similarities between their
native Tuscany & the wine-growing landscape of
Napa Valley.
Although he became interested in wine growing only

7

in America. Only after they moved to St. Helena, after he bought his first funeral home, when he became a non-denominational undertaker. Before he became a father: of twins.

& a 24-year-old fashion designer, leaving her first fall collection ———— her aunt Laura's unfinished portrait of her, wearing a sample suit from her first fall collection, an ankle-long sea-green velvet skirt with a short close-fitting jacket of the same material, riding her black stallion Chopin.

The stallion had been a wedding present from her aunt Laura. Who was a painter, & a breeder of horses. & an avid reader of D.H. Lawrence; in the English original.

She used to keep Chopin in her aunt's stables, on her aunt's estate outside Fiesole. Where she had lived between 15 & 18, after the death of her parents in a car accident. She'd spent most of her married weekends riding her horse, with or without her husband of a little over 1 year.

————Posing for her aunt Laura's Gothic-novel image of her, that was to be a publicity poster for her first fall collection. At that time, in the Italian mid-thirties, her aunt Laura's portraits of elongated young women with Modigliani necks & streaming black or red hair, riding black or white stallions, the women's hair intertwining with the manes of the horses had become extremely fashionable.

She resented leaving her horse behind, when they were taking all their furniture along on this absurd American adventure.

Which was the first deep disagreement between them: She had no congenital memory of persecutions. But of respect, for merchants who had come to Italy with silk

worms concealed in their robes. Who had settled, &
bred wealth.

Whose grandsons *&* granddaughters had become
artists. Painting alchemists, who blended lead with
gold, in reputed workshops. Who illuminated the
great books of their time.

She was the niece, & granddaughter, & great-great-
great-granddaughter of Italians, whose sole religion
was art. She had never thought of herself as Jewish.
She refused to believe that her friends & neighbors
would start discriminating against her all of a sudden,
because a bunch of raving maniacs suddenly decreed
that she was not Italian.

—Which they were sure to do   more & more bluntly;
with more & more convincing rationalizations: her
husband of a little over 1 year assured her. Quoting the
example of his ancestors, who had also had friends &
neighbors. Who had watched them burn, & drown.

Her aunt Laura's estate outside Fiesole was converted
into a playground for fascist dignitaries, late in 1943.
After her aunt Laura hanged herself from a tie beam in
one of her stables, after she shot every 1 of her horses, including the left-behind Chopin: as the mother
found out after the end of the war. From a Mrs. Linati,
a close friend of her aunt's whom she'd known since
girlhood & who had been present at her wedding. To
whom she finally wrote when all her letters to her aunt
Laura remained unanswered.

When her husband of almost 1 decade asked her to
forgive him for having been right. & urged her to take
up riding again...

She still considers herself Italian rather than Jewish.
Florentine, since their move to St. Helena, where the

local Italian is Americanized Calabrese, or Neapoli-
tan, or Sicilian. A strange new language that mixes
past & present, & says *stima* (respect) to mean steam
(*vapore*).
Although lately   when asked   she has been telling
recent acquaintances that she is French.

—That's what she told the juvenile sportswear manufacturer, who asked her about her background. After
she was introduced to him by their neighbor Marcia
Campbell. Marcia Campbell's bushy eyebrows regis-
tered surprise upon hearing her Italian neighbor of
close to 30 years say that she was French...   (To
improve her image as a fashion designer in the eyes of
an American manufacturer of juvenile sportswear?)
To avoid being classified   socially misclassified   as
an Italian immigrant, in America.
Where she buried her career   her sense of style; most
of her aesthetic satisfactions   in her husband's non-
denominational funeral parlor, when they moved to
St. Helena from San Francisco. When she was pregnant with the twins.
Although lately she has been trying to become a fashion designer again: of sportswear for children.

> Together they are almost
> as old as their furniture:
> 70 & 66 respectively.
> —The visiting daughter is
> 31.—   Their postures
> are extensions of the
> high-backed dignity of
> their chairs, on which
> they have sat for over a
> generation of dinners,

                    passing the salt across 10
                    feet of highly polished
                    greyness.
                    Inverting positions would
                    be as inconceivable as a
                    sex change.

At least that is how they look to the visiting daughter:
Immutable.

Although, every once in a while, she thinks she is picking up silent signals from the father's short end of the
table; on her right. A sighed plea to let bygones be
bygones. To be forgiven, perhaps. For something that
had perhaps happened long ago. Too long ago for the
visiting daughter to have witnessed.

Or perhaps for something the visiting daughter *has*
witnessed. For as long as she can remember. Something she used to sit across from at the dinner table &
next to in school & sleep in the same room with, every
day of her life, until she left for college, a little over 12
years ago.

Something for which she, too, used to long to be forgiven sometimes: her twin sister Laura's deformity...

                    The mother sits taller
                    than the father, despite
                    an age-humped back.
                    Because of her hair,
                    perhaps   still thick; still
                    a rich bluish black
                    which tops her head like
                    an imperial crown.

The visiting daughter doesn't remember ever seeing
the mother with her hair down. Not even in the middle

of childhood nights, when she'd wake up & see the mother bending over Laura's bed. Holding a glass to Laura's lips, after another operation.

> Perhaps the father has
> shrunk, due to the stroke
> he suffered 8 months ago.
> Which has added a slight
> slur to his speech & given
> a somewhat devious slant
> to his large biblical fea-
> tures.
> He still looks imposing,
> though. ____At least to
> the visiting daughter.
> ____& his back is
> straight, braced against
> the high back of his chair.

To the mother, he has looked devious for the last 26½ years. When she first began to think of him as: the unctuous undertaker. After he refused to sign her out of the mental institution to which she had committed herself, in a drunken fit of depression, after the fifth unsuccessful operation on her daughter Laura's spine. When Laura was not quite 4½ years old.

When the unctuous undertaker, the former Italian doctor, from Florence, convinced the other doctors at the mental institution that his poor dear wife had a drinking problem. Which "they" had been battling with for the last 4 years or so. Since shortly after the birth of their twin daughters. Which had been a diffi-cult birth.

...Which had cost his poor dear wife her romantic long black hair. That used to stream behind her like a

dark silk scarf when she rode her horses, English sad-
dle, through the Umbrian countryside.

...He had wept when he'd found her beautiful hair
strewn all over the pillow, after the delivery. & had
gathered it up, painfully, strand by strand, before she
regained full consciousness. He'd had it made into a
wig, ready for her to wear by the time she was able to
get out of bed...

His grieved undertaker's mouth has been repulsive to
her ever since. Telling lies which she couldn't disprove
without appearing to be paranoid. If not insane: Why
would this visibly concerned husband lie about the
loss of her hair...

Which was, moreover, a fact: She had been as bald as
her newly-born little Laura, after the birth of the
twins. But *he* hadn't known about it. She had managed
to hide her naked scalp for 6 weeks from him &
everybody else with twisted towels & kerchiefs,
until she could get a wig made that looked exactly like
her old hair.
—It had taken a lot longer to get a wig custom made,
than the 7½ days she'd stayed in bed after the birth of
the twins.

He hadn't even believed that she'd lost her hair,
because it had grown back   —but kinky; with greying patches—   by the time he found out that she was
wearing a wig.
Which she'd been wearing for over 4 years, when he
found out. When it came off in his fists, during one of
his earlier rages, when he grabbed her by the hair to
shake her into agreeing with his indisputably superior
medical wisdom   —after all, he hadn't always been

an undertaker!— that Laura needed another the
fifth operation on her 4½-year-old spine.

She hadn't read about Mary Stuart's execution then,
about Mary Stuart's wig coming off in the fist of her
executioner: as Antonia Fraser describes it in her
book. The book was a Christmas present from Laura,
when it first came out, 16, maybe 17 years after the
incident with the wig. —Which is only one of the
many similarities she keeps discovering between herself and Mary Stuart.
Who was also 5'11" tall. & had had striking hair in her
youth. & had loved horses. & both of them certainly
had been a great deal better off before they married.
She has only one husband to Mary's three: the sickly-
sweet dauphin of France, the peacock Darnley, & his
murderer Bothwell. But the difference between Mary's
first (boy-) husband & the worst of the other two
combined cannot have been much greater than the
difference between the young Italian doctor she had
married with a lavishness worthy of royalty; on her
aunt Laura's estate outside Fiesole & the unctuous
American undertaker who tried to keep her impris-
oned. Exactly like Mary Stuart.

She is finding it harder & harder to face him across the
dinner table. Especially when he puts on his loving-
husband-&-father act, whenever he has an audience.
He is putting it on right now, full blast, for the visiting
daughter.
Who is eating it all up.
Who would refuse to believe that the unctuous undertaker, her doting daddy with the slurry speech, tried to
have his wife, her mother, locked up in a boobyhatch,
26½ years ago, to keep her out of his way while he

screwed every hole within his reach. Who would think that her mother had gone off her rocker, to be using the language she's using. In reference to her loving daddy who just had a stroke.

Maybe her mother has been nuts for a long time. Maybe her daddy was right when he tried to have her committed...

She tries to see   & especially to hear   him as little as feasible. His slurry labored speech assaults her aesthetic sense. Which may be over-developed, because of the emphasis on art in her upbringing.

& because she sees & hears him for what he is, unscreened by affection: a self-indulgent old body that is falling apart.

That has been an inexhaustible source of humiliation to her for almost 1/2 of her life, blocking the fulfillment of every passion/ or talent/ or self-respect she once had, & yet she is expected to take care of that old body. By everybody. Including the deteriorating, increasingly repulsive old body.

—Although, since his stroke, she thinks she detects a slurry undertone of doubt when he plays the lovey-dovey hubby-daddy for his audiences.

Even his private rages have a different ring. As though he had begun to wonder if she might perhaps unexpectedly not take care of him. If she might perhaps take care of him the way he took care of her 26½ years ago, & let him rot in an institution, while she lived a life of her own. Watching him fall apart, while everybody else thought she was taking loving care of him. As everybody else was expecting her to do: Their daughters. Their friends & neighbors. All the people who knew them in St. Helena, California.

Where she is known as 1/2   the lesser-known 1/2
of a couple:

...Elderly. Italian. *Northern* Italian: they speak Dante's language, even though they have no head of Dante
on their sideboard in their diningroom.

...They don't even have a sideboard in their diningroom.

...In which they eat all their meals, even though
there's only the two of them now, since the girls went
off to college.

...Which was a relief to the whole neighborhood.
When the traffic of boys in cars & on bicycles finally
let up, on the road to their house on the hill. & their
screen door finally stopped slamming.

...You wouldn't have thought those girls would be so
popular, what with one being kind of ordinary looking, & the other a cripple. A hunchback. A *gobba*.
With a face like an angel's, & gorgeous hair. Still: you
didn't want to get caught passing her on the left.
Gobba di sinistra brought bad luck...

...Everything is quiet now. Just the elderly Italian
couple alone in their big 100-year-old stone house on
the hill: the lesser-known wife, taking care of her
better-known   better-liked   husband...

She'd like to see those people's faces if she told them
she hates the old lecher's guts.

...Who is holding up remarkably, after his stroke.
Which isn't surprising. He's always had stamina. Not
too proud to work with his hands   as an embalmer
when they first came over. & after having been a medical doctor, in the old country...

...He's retired now, bless his heart. Likes to grow his

own wine. That has always been his hobby. That's
why he moved the family to Napa Valley. To St.
Helena. To be able to grow his own wine...

——For the name, actually: St. Helena. Wine growing
had come as an afterthought, suggested by the neg-
lected vineyard behind the house.
He enjoys the rewriting of European history in American place names. & savors the reminder of Napoleon's
exile   titanic aspirations softened by gardening   in
the taste of his wine.——

...Good wine, too. They've all had a chance to try it,
at one time or another. Because that's how he is:
generous. & outgoing. A pleasant old gentleman with
a twinkle in his eye...

A sour-graping tyrant who gloats over Napoleon's
defeat.
Who turns into a screaming maniac when he's alone
with his wife. When there's no one around to hear
him.
Who chased his wife around the house with a
corkscrew in his fist, when she declined to taste his
new wine. Causing her to fall & hurt her right hand &
knee, when she tried to get away from him. When she
tried to run out the back door, over to their backyard
neighbor Marcia Campbell; not so long ago. No later
than 2 days ago, last Saturday afternoon.
He is forever thinking up tricks to make her doubt her
sanity.—Hiding all their knives for a week, & then
surreptitiously returning them to their customary
places in the kitchen cupboard, for instance. Pretend-
ing that they'd been there all along. To make her think
that she must be imagining things   that she may be

imagining the things he does to her, has done to her for over 1/4 of a century, to prevent her from telling someone —their backyard neighbor Marcia Campbell— how his character changes when they're alone in the house.

Not even her daughters know how violent he can be. They would refuse to believe that their Dad threatened her with a corkscrew even if she were to show them her bruises. Even Laura would refuse to believe her. It's diabolical how he controls his rages in front of others. The diabolical method of madness: trying to prove his own sanity by making her doubt hers.
To prove that he was right, 26½ years ago, when he refused to sign her out.   —Why don't you stay a little longer. You need the rest: he had said to her. In front of the diplomatically nodding doctors. —Don't worry about the girls. I found a splendid nurse who's looking after all three of us...Smiles. Smiles. A loving peck on her cheek, as he rose to walk out on her. A man-to-man handshake with the doctors; a pledge of professional allegiance: After all, he used to be a doctor himself, in Florence, Italy, before "Mussolini switched him from the supplying to the receiving end of the line": as he still likes to say when someone expresses admiration for the social flexibility of a former doctor turned undertaker.

She can't remember when he first began to make her squirm. The odiously jovial undertaker who screams at her at home has completely obliterated whoever it was she had once married.

Of course he'd been sleeping with the splendid nurse when she came back from the mental institution.

When she finally did get out. After sending an S.O.S. to her aunt's old friend Mrs. Linati. Who was the only person she had left in this world who was her friend more than his.
Who flew over from Florence, & passed herself off as her aunt to be allowed to take her home.

It wasn't his adultery that bothered her. She had no desire to sleep with him ever again after his refusal to sign her out. How could she open her body to a man who had tried to have her put away.
What bothered her was his telling her that the splendid nurse had used her injector & her contraceptive foam. ...In an emergency... after all they hadn't planned on sleeping together. It had simply come over them, sitting across from each other night after night, after the twins had been put to bed. It was too late to drive to a pharmacy when it came over them. All the pharmacies were closed. & understandably, neither of them wanted to take chances...

& understandably he waited to tell her about the injector —about which he was telling her out of consideration for her: she probably preferred to buy a new one— until after old Mrs. Linati had flown back to Florence. After he'd charmed old Mrs. Linati into questioning the need for her rescue mission, in response to a cry for help from inside a mental institution. —Where the mentally exhausted mother of 5-year-old twins one of them in constant need of medical attention was finally getting the rest (the drying out) she desperately needed...— Over many glasses of his proudest wine, in the sunset corner of the porch, while the mentally exhausted sober mother put the twins to bed, after preparing a special last supper for old Mrs. Linati, to whom she owed her freedom.

—Who seemed to remember, during dinner, that Aunt Laura used to be awfully fond of *grappa*.

—& hadn't her parents' fatal car accident been ascribed to drunken driving...

Who didn't protest, the next morning, when they were alone in the car, on the way to the airport, when the released mental patient expressed the   painful   feeling that: He had won! That her dear Aunt Laura's closest friend, her only surviving ally in this world, no longer believed her either.

Who had a look of fear in her eyes   as though she distrusted the released mental patient's driving because the car was swerving slightly just then.

She'd driven back from the airport, rehearsing her divorce. Planning her divorced life: as a New York fashion designer, raising her girls by herself, without him even knowing where they lived.

But her 5-year-old twins were standing in the driveway when she pulled in. & Laura smiled her angel's smile, & said: "We're so glad you're home, Mother. Now we're the right four of us again."

He had probably stage-managed the scene, to lead up to the bigger scene he had planned for later that night. When he knelt at her feet   in the bedroom they'd still been sharing then; which is his bedroom now   weeping large tears, begging her to forget the nurse. Who had been nothing but a geographical coincidence. Because the house had felt so lonely without her... Making her almost believe that he meant it. Because she wanted to believe it. That he'd had a change of heart, which she didn't want to challenge by bringing up the mental institution.

& the next evening Laura had thrown her thin little

arms around her neck & said: "I haven't had any pain
anywhere all day. I'm so glad we're the right four of us
again."

For a while they had been almost happy. At least she'd
thought they were, lying close to each other in the
center of the bed, falling asleep holding hands.

She was slowly forgetting the injector incident, thinking that she'd soon be able to use the new one he had
bought for her; when the screaming started up again.
In the kitchen in the middle of the morning, when she
returned from driving the girls to kindergarden.

When she found out that he'd been consoling a recent
widow. From him: screaming that it was her doing if
he slept with other women. Her carrying on like an
injured queen. Did she take him for some kind of
eunuch, who was thrilled & grateful to hold her
majesty's hand.

She'd run upstairs, to get away from his voice. &
started moving her things out of the bedroom into the
unused maid's room down the hall. Where she has
been sleeping ever since.

She was pushing her rosewood dresser down the hall
when he came up after her, still screaming, & picked
up one of the drawers she'd pulled out, & smashed it
on the floor, 1/2" from her feet.

That afternoon she'd bought the diary. To keep a
record of the unbelievable things he said & did to her
when they were alone. To prove to herself that he had
really said & done these things, that she had not
invented them, dreamt them during recurring night-
mares, when she'd find him sitting on the porch not
long after a scene, all smiles & thoughtfulness, pour-
ing a glass of wine to a visitor. To their backyard
neighbor Marcia Campbell of whom he'd never been

overly fond. Or in the kitchen, making a pot of espresso for their daughters who'd just come home from school.

Perhaps her daughters would find her diary, after she died. Or perhaps she'd mail it to them   to Laura, at her law office in L.A.   to be opened after she died.

Before him, as she'd always been sure she would. Until recently, until he had his stroke.

When her daughters would finally find out how she had lived, next to this man who was their father. When they would perhaps realize what kind of husband their father had been.

—Years of recorded nastiness, & ruses, & duplicity, each with its date; in some cases even the hour & duration, to convey abolute time-objective truthfulness to the reader. She'd kept the diary hidden under a stack of old fashion sketches in the right bottom drawer of her rosewood dresser in her bedroom.

& should have taken it with her when she went to stay with Laura in L.A. for 3 weeks, to help Laura move into her new apartment, 3 years ago.

At his urging.   —Because he was still sleeping around? At age 67? Or had he, too, sensed his increasing lack of control? Which she had been sensing, during his increasingly frequent rages. & wanted to get her out of the house before he finally killed her?   — Thereby annulling over 1/4 of a century of careful hypocrisy...

Which he had apparently suspected her of recording, for almost 1/4 of a century.

Which had not occurred to her.

It had not occurred to her that he might be suspicious of her. He had no reason to be suspicious of her: *She* had not tried to have him committed.

She should have realized the deviousness of a guilty conscience: sending her to L.A. so that he could invade her bedroom & search through her dresser drawers. & destroy the daily evidence she had accumulated against him during 1/4 of a century.

She should have taken her diary with her & left the evidence with Laura. In a sealed envelope, to be opened after her death. Because, when she returned to St. Helena & opened her right bottom dresser drawer to record the volcanic welcome scene he made her
—because she had not announced her arrival, but had arrived home unannounced, after 10 P.M.—
which her daughters, & their backyard neighbor Marcia Campbell, & all the people who knew them in L.A., & San Francisco, & St. Helena, would refuse to believe if she tried to tell them about it, but might believe if they read it in her diary after her death
____after he finally killed her; bodily or otherwise: what difference did it make____
her diary had disappeared. Just like the knives, but unlike the knives it never reappeared.

—Not unlike the letters Mary Stuart thought she'd been writing in secret, which were intercepted by her jailer, & decoded before they were sent on to Mary's friends & allies. Incriminating them & her. In devious preparation for Mary's execution...

The visiting daughter thinks she is picking up swishing sounds of a veil being lowered over the mind of the mother, at the short end of the table to her left. Shutting out the father's silent pleas.

The visiting daughter doesn't know that the mother

has begun to identify the father with Mary Stuart's last
jailer, the righteous puritan Sir (Sir!) Amyas Paulet.
_____Who also shrank from outright murder, mean-
while making Mary's life unlivable. Depriving &
degrading her in every devious way he could imagine.
Suggesting that she go horseback riding once again
—straight into the fateful set-up for her trial & decapitation.
The unctuous undertaker also used to urge her to take
up riding again, in America   —always in front of an
audience—   but then he'd balk in private if she mentioned the price of boots...

The visiting daughter doesn't know that the mother
keeps Antonia Fraser's *Mary Queen of Scots* on the
table next to her bed. She's never been inside the
mother's bedroom, where no one was allowed to go
when she & Laura were still living at home.
She doesn't know that Laura gave Antonia Fraser's
biography of Mary Stuart to the mother as a Christmas present, when the book first came out. When the
visiting daughter had started her drift from place to
place.
The mother had not particularly liked Mary Stuart at
first, because of her condescension toward a Florentine merchant's daughter: Catherine de Medicis.
—Who became Mary's mother-in-law, & ceremoni-
ously stepped aside to let the 16-year-old queen enter
the church before her. But then stepped back in front
of her again when Mary was widowed, at 17½.—
Which used to make the mother laugh. It was only
after reading about Mary's wig, at the end of the book,
during Mary's decapitation, that the mother discovered all the other similarities between them.

Unlike either parent the
visiting daughter sits
slouched over her plate.
A plump dot, equidistant
from the 2 short ends of
the table, like the tip of a
triangle.
If her twin sister Laura
had come home for
Christmas, they'd be
forming a family square.
Her twin sister Laura had
always sat at the other
long side of the long,
highly polished grey mar-
ble dining table. Those
had been their places
since their highchair
days. Inverting positions
would have been as
inconceivable as switch-
ing bodies.

For which the visiting "normal" daughter used to
wish sometimes, during their adolescence...

_____Why?
Had she felt jealous of her handicapped twin, as a
child? Because of the extra care & attention which
parents/teachers/doctors/nurses had lavished on her
twin, because of her handicap? the psychiatrist had
asked.
The visiting daughter had been sent to see the school
psychiatrist, by the dean, after a dormitory roommate

refused to pose for her in drawing class. The roommate "didn't like to be stared at by a girl who tried to
crawl into bed with her & fondle her."
That's what the roommate had said to the painter who
conducted the workshop. A new artist-in-residence
who had just arrived on campus & couldn't know that
the roommate had been upset by an earlier drawing
the visiting daughter had made of her.

Jealous! Of all the pains Laura had had to endure as a
child!   Seven operations.   Which had neither
straightened her spine nor strengthened her breakable
legs. No! God no! How could any body be jealous of
that!
Then why____?
Perhaps because they were twins. Not identical twins,
but they'd always been close.
She sometimes felt that she ought to share Laura's
burdens. They had always shared everything else:
Their room. Their friends. Their combs & brushes.
Books.
—Montaigne, with whom they fell in love   both of
them, simultaneously   on their 16th birthday.
Laura had been given Montaigne by their mother. &
she had been given Dante by their father. They hadn't
cared for Dante too much, but they'd both loved Mon-
taigne.
They used to read his essays out loud to each other.
Reading each other to sleep. Dreaming twin dreams of
captive birds in a white stucco-&-wire bird palace in
Montaigne's garden in Bordeaux. "The birds inside
trying to get out. The birds outside trying to get in."

The visiting daughter didn't know   she still doesn't
know   that her twin sister Laura's interest in Mon-

taigne had been sparked by a fascination/identifi-
cation with Ninon de Lanclos, the witty 17th-century
Frenchwoman who decided "to live like a man" rather
than accept the "role of silent suffering" she had
watched other 17th-century Frenchwomen around
her accept —her retaliatingly pious mother—
while she grew up.

Who was one of the many early feminists whom history ususally dismisses with a badge of dishonor. Or a
shrug. Or with disdainful silence. But who was lov-
ingly disinterred letter by lover by lawsuit & vin-
dicated by the 20th-century French historian Emile
Magne. Whose imagination she had seduced post-
humously.

Laura had been given Emile Magne's definitive biography of Ninon de Lanclos by their French teacher.

Unknown to her twin. Who happened to be elsewhere,
when she began to read the book.

Which Laura continued to read silently; in secret
whenever her twin was away, attending an art class, or
at the gym.

Which Laura kept hidden from her twin & everybody else behind the Italian Bible in the parents'
bookshelf. —The book least likely to be pulled out
by the atheist parents.— & kept rereading, unknown to her twin & everybody else.

Although perhaps not totally unknown to the mother:
Montaigne had been the favorite author of Ninon de
Lanclos. At least during Ninon's youth...

The visiting daughter has no idea that her deformed
twin sister lived a separate, secret life as a 17th-century
Parisian courtesan, during their shared adolescence.

——College was their first separation: Laura was
studying law in Boston, & she had come to New York

to study art. They had never been separated before...

Who knew what she had perhaps done to her twin
sister, inside their mother? To come out weighing 5 lbs
when Laura had weighed 2 lbs, 2½ ounces...
Perhaps she had kicked her twin sister in the spine   to
kick her out of her way, to get out faster...   She had
been born first: 12 minutes ahead of Laura...

_____What nonsense! What criminal adult had planted
such absurdities in her head!

No one. No one had said anything.
Ever.

_____You can always tell that you've run out of the
good seed when you start turning them out runty like
that: an old Italian neighbor had said to the mother,
whom she'd met pushing the 1-year-old Laura home
from a visit to the doctor.
O, she's a twin, no wonder: the old woman had said:
You make sure you don't let them near each other, you
hear, or the strong one will suck the life out of the runt.
They've got only one soul between them, you know, &
the strong one is sure to try & grab it all for herself...
The mother had repeated the old woman's 30-year-
old remark to the visiting daughter in the kitchen earlier that morning. Imitating the old woman's thick
Italian English. With a grimace: The mother has
worked hard on her English.
_____At age 1, Laura's head had been the size of an egg:
the mother had said, cracking an egg on the edge of the
mixing bowl, for the Spanish cream she was making
for dessert for their Christmas dinner. & just as bald.
It wasn't until Laura turned 3   between 2 & 3   that

she started to grow her lovely hair. The kind of hair
their grand-aunt Laura had liked to paint: a rich
copper glow. Which had come out as a pale orange
fuzz, at first...

Whereas the visiting daughter had started growing
her   stringy   hair much earlier, between 1 & 2.

The visiting daughter had always seemed to be 1 year
ahead of Laura. Physically. As though her 12-minute
edge over Laura kept translating itself into months,
after their birth.

Laura had always been exceptionally alert, though.
Right from the start. Which had always made the
mother ask herself how keenly the baby was feeling
her pains.

Had the visiting daughter any idea how the mother
used to suffer with Laura, through every new operation? How a child's deformity affects a mother?
Always that torturing background thought that she
had perhaps done something to cause the deformity...

—Having intercourse during her pregnancy, for
instance.

On which their father had insisted almost nightly,
because they didn't have to take precautions, now that
"it" had already happened anyway.

Which had perhaps hurt the fetus...   Although: why
would it have hurt only one, & not both...

—Did the visiting daughter know that Mary Stuart
had also had twins by her third & most abject of
husbands, Bothwell. Mary Stuart had miscarried her
twins, & after that she'd led a life of total chastity,
although she'd been only 25 at the time...

The visiting daughter didn't know. Or care. She has
never been particularly interested in Mary Stuart.

Who seemed to have been another well-haired woman
her grandaunt might have liked to paint on a horse.
If she had felt more at home in the mother's kitchen
she might have expressed her surprise at the mother's
apparent sympathy with a historical bigot.
—Mother! What's happening to your atheist faith...
Something Laura might feel at home enough to say to
the mother. Would certainly have said to the mother
12 years ago, before they left for college.
The visiting daughter has been wondering if Laura still
says & does the kind of things she used to think up
when they'd both been teenagers. Or if becoming a
successful lawyer has turned her into a cautious con-
formist, despite her nonconformist body.
—Which would be considered art, if Laura were a
sculpture. Lifted beyond practical considerations,
such as mobility, or reproducing...

_____Was she perhaps trying to prove that her
deformed twin sister was desirable, by trying to make
love to the roommate? A girl who also slept in the
same room with her, as her twin sister had done until
recently? the college psychiatrist had asked.
Because she hadn't told the college psychiatrist that
the roommate had been upset by the earlier drawing
she had made of her. During an earlier class; with a
different teacher.
Which he would probably not have believed.   —The
roommate had horse teeth. & bared her gums when
she smiled.—
Nor would he probably have believed that her
deformed twin sister was beautiful.
Which he would probably have interpreted as another
guilt-inspired fantasy   looking at her "normal" face
& her "normal"   —stringy—   hair   since twins are

expected to look alike. Even when they're not identical twins they're expected to resemble each other to some extent.

Laura's face resembled no one. Except perhaps a Boticelli. Or a legendary heroine. A star. Her hair was a legend all its own: thick, long, & silky. It always looked as though the sun had got caught in it.

Would the college psychiatrist have believed that it was for Laura that their classmates used to come to their hilltop house in St. Helena?   —Beleaguering the place. "It's like having a bitch in heat in the house": the mother would say in disgust. Not believing either that it was her deformed daughter   Laura   whom "those boys" (& men) came to see. Seeing only that it was with her other   normal   daughter that they tried to make out.

Afterwards. After they had talked themselves into an erection with Laura. Whom they didn't dare touch. Who looked too fragile, romantically out of reach, sitting in a corner of the couch. Her breakable legs tucked under her; the hump on her back hidden under a copper curtain of hair.

—Being Ninon de Lanclos. (Unknown to her twin, the visiting   normal   daughter.) Holding Ninon de Lanclos' famed salon in 17th-century Paris   36, rue de la Tournelle   while sitting on the parental couch in St. Helena, 20th-century California.

The visiting daughter knows next to nothing about Ninon de Lanclos. She still doesn't know that the boys & men (some of them married men: their French teacher, one of their father's hearse drivers, their father's bookkeeper) who'd straddle her under a bush

in the backyard or in the back of their cars, after talking with Laura _____silently designated by Laura as
being worthy of straddling her, by a raised eyebrow,
an inviting smile_____ were chosen for resemblances
with Ninon de Lanclos' many lovers.

With whose physical & character traits Laura had
become intimately familiar.

Whom she'd favor capriciously: 1 day yes, the next
day no _____via her normal twin sister, the visiting,
normal daughter_____ in imitation of "the male pre-
rogative of choice" which her 17th-century role model
had arrogated to herself as soon as she was old enough
to have lovers. Having watched her virtue-rewarded
mother sigh through decades of Ninon's father's
spirited escapades _____Ninon's father's much pub-
licized grand extramarital passion for the lawyer's
wife Lucrèce de Gouges, whom he had known as a
little girl_____ to the accomplished accompaniment
of his lute.

The visiting daughter still doesn't know or understand why her twin sister Laura insisted on giving
their father a lute for his 57th birthday.

On which he has never played. Which he keeps in his
bedroom, next to the medals he has won for his wine.
She has never questioned Laura's reason for buying
the lute. _____Which had seemed like a wonderful
birthday present for their 57-year-old father. Wonder-
fully unexpected._____ Not any more than she has
questioned Laura's unpredictable choice of lovers.

Who had all been & stayed in love with Laura.
Not with her.

Who'd keep their eyes tightly closed over their image
of Laura, while straddling the substitute.

In stony silence.

Or else, they'd ask her to talk to them. Talk...talk...

just keep talking... because the unidentical twins had one resemblance that fooled everybody even their parents: They had absolutely identical voices.

—Both parents thought that it was Laura calling them from the airport, the evening before. Although both parents knew that Laura was spending this Christmas in southern Portugal.

_____It's the first time that Laura hasn't come home for Christmas.____ Which the visiting daughter hadn't known, or she might not have come either. ____For the first time in over 12 years.____ She had come to see Laura. To talk with Laura, with whom she hasn't talked in over 12 years. —Except once, by telephone long distance; collect.— Everybody she'd known until she left home had always wanted to talk with Laura.

On the wall across from the visiting daughter, equidistant from the absent Laura's customary place at the other long side of the dinner table, two paternal ancestors in their prime a large-featured male, holding a jewel-encrusted snuff box, & a bare-shouldered female, surfacing from a waterfall of lace stare past each other from gold-leafed oval frames.

(Once the mother scotchtaped a pair of sunglasses

onto the male ancestor's
prominent nose. To
amuse her daughter
Laura, who was recover-
ing from another opera-
tion on her spine.
—& couldn't yet turn her
head: which she would
have had to do, to see the
glasses from where she
was sitting, propped on
pillows.—
The glasses had not
amused the father. Who
had removed them.)

A dank flannel silence
hangs over the meal,
punctured by the nervous
scribbling of the mother's
fork in her plate, & by the
father's throaty swallows
of wine.

The visiting daughter wishes for a magic word to
break the deadlock between the parents. Which must
have existed between the parents for as long as she can
remember, but it feels more oppressive than she had
remembered:

The mother doesn't
speak to the father. &
when the father starts to
say something
        other than a throaty

request for more: duck/
orange sauce/sauteed
ferns/Spanish cream   all
of a high gourmet qual-
ity, conscientiously pre-
pared by the mother who
strives for perfection in
everything she does: her
cooking/her English/her
fashion sketches/her
driving/her embroidery,
which the mother took
up when she began iden-
tifying with Mary Stuart
      & for economy: the
visiting daughter remem-
bers wishing for more
of everything   as an ado-
lescent. Unlike her absent
twin sister Laura the visiting daughter has inher-
ited the father's tendency
to indulge in second help-
ings, & the subsequent
tendency toward plump-
ness
the mother gets up &
leaves the room.

_____His recent speech
impediment offends her:
the father stage-whispers
to the visiting daughter.
Who protests: His speech
is fine. She has under-

stood every word she's
heard him say since her
arrival the evening
before. Even over the
phone she'd understood
him, when she'd called
from the airport.
But he insists : The
mother has told him so
herself. He disgusts her
now. Perhaps he has
always disgusted her...

The visiting daughter is
still protesting when the
mother returns, carrying
a second   small   bowl
of Spanish cream. Which
she places between the
father & the visiting
daughter, equidistant
from their elbows on the
dinner table.

A gesture which the visiting daughter interprets as a
manifesto, on the mother's part: Not only does the
mother not wish any more Spanish cream for herself,
although she served herself only the smallest spoonful,
but she is disciplined   & trim   unlike the father &
the visiting daughter, but she is also fully aware of   &
not surprised by   the father's attempt to turn the visiting daughter against her. The instant she left the room.
They're sitting at her dinner table like two   over-
indulging   accomplices.

The mother is no fool. She has watched him work his
persuasion tactics on each & every person who set
foot in their house since the day the evening he
won old Mrs. Linati over to his side, 26½ years ago.
Making old Mrs. Linati doubt that he'd been trying to
have his wife put away in the insane asylum. Making
her ordeal look like a loving husband's emergency
measure of concern. & like paranoia on her part.
Even their daughters have always loved their father
better than they love their mother. Even her absent
daughter Laura.

Lately he has been working on their backyard neighbor Marcia Campbell. A 50-some-year-old painter,
who earns her living as a legal secretary. Who lives in
the converted hot house in back of them. With 14 cats.
He's never had much use for cats, but a week ago he
bought a cat painting from their backyard neighbor,
"to show 'their' gratitude" after their backyard neighbor introduced her to the juvenile sportswear manufacturer for whom she has started sketching children's
ski suits.
Marcia Campbell had been the only person in St.
Helena who'd been *her* friend more than his. The only
living soul to whom she'd dare hint about his fits of
violence from time to time.
To which Marcia Campbell had always responded
with sympathy & understanding. —Ultimately with
the introduction to the sportswear manufacturer. Saying that: the mother's life made her realize how much
better off she was, as a single woman. Even if she had
to work as a legal secretary to support her painting.
But recently, after he bought one of her   —larger—
paintings Marcia raises her bushy eyebrows at the

slightest mention of anything negative connected with him.
—Wives often envy the freedom of the working woman, but are afraid to take the risk: Marcia Campbell had said to her 2 days ago, last Saturday afternoon, when she'd run over to Marcia Campbell's house, to get away from him chasing her with his corkscrew. .
About which she had hinted to Marcia Campbell: in case she wasn't able to meet the juvenile sportswear manufacturer's first deadline. Because she had hurt her drawing hand, running from her husband. & she wanted her first batch of sketches to be perfect...
—Even if they were only fashion sketches...only for children...even if she wasn't a real artist, unlike Marcia Campbell...
Who had replied   with bushily contracted eyebrows   that excessive preoccupation with perfection could sometimes be a way of avoiding one's commitment. Which made the only difference...in her opinion commitment made the only difference...between a "real" &   she assumed   an "unreal" artist...The mother was strictly on her own, as far as the juvenile sportswear manufacturer was concerned: Marcia Campbell had said: She had introduced them, & that was all she could be expected to do. She couldn't be expected to apologize to him for the mother's private life, if the mother was late with her sketches...

The visiting daughter wonders how a wise person
—the gynecologist Claire Fontaine—   would deal with two mature people   —mature is a euphemism; they're old: 70 & 66 respectively. The lean mother has begun to grow chipmunk cheeks—   who are not

speaking to each other across their highly polished grey marble dinner table.

—Which is important to both of them. Both parents take pride in the authenticity of their funiture. Their china/their crystal/their food/their wine. The antique silver bowl with fresh white roses.   —Which do look beautiful, on the shiny grey marble surface.—   In their house. In their landscape: Napa Valley reminded both parents separately of Umbria, the evening before in the twilight, shortly after the arrival of the visiting daughter.

Would the wise Claire knock their old heads together. & tell them: to knock it off. That they're too old to be so childish. To take themselves so childishly seriously, no matter what justifiable grudge each bears against the other. To laugh it away, & enjoy their beautiful landscape/old stone house/authentic belongings. To enjoy each other! because they'll both be dead before they know it...

& because of the blunt authority of wisdom the parents would feel ridiculous.

They'd slowly start smiling at each other sheepishly across the long slab of polished greyness. & slowly get up & slowly walk toward each other   —each walking exactly 1/2 the distance around the long side of the table—   with outstretched arms. & hug, for the first time in 20, perhaps 30 years. & bury as many years of steadily accumulated, steadily hardened grudges under an avalanche of laughter.

Unless the parents' grudge-bearing is the incentive that has been keeping them alive. Each planning to outlive

the other: Thereby proving the other's final admission
that the survivor was right. All along.
& would the survivor go on a guilt trip then? &
canonize the suddenly flawless departed. & spend her/
his remaining life in equally joyless repentance: If I
only...If only I...

Unless the visiting daughter is misreading the parents'
non-speaking silence as joylessness. Perhaps they
derive satisfaction from their tacit warfare. & count
each new grudge as a point. & add up their scores each
night, chuckling to themselves, in their separate
rooms, in their separate antique beds.

Which the wise Claire would have sensed. Instantly.
Upon sitting down at the table between them.
—Where no wise person would probably sit down in
the first place.—
Or else, the wise person would quietly enjoy the
meal   —although perhaps declining the duck, if the
wise person is a strict vegetarian like Claire—   & get
up & leave. With a friendly goodnight, & a compli-
ment about the quality of the food & the wine. &
perhaps the fresh white roses. But no further explanation.
As the visiting daughter feels tempted to do. Intensely
wishing for a phone call from New York that would
give her a pretext for leaving. Although she arrived
only the evening before, & had told the parents that
she'd be staying the full week, until New Year's day.
—Which was short enough: in the unanimous,
though separately voiced opinion of both parents.
Who hadn't seen her in over 12 years. & thought the
flight was too expensive for just 1 short week...

The visiting daughter sits
in closed-eyed concentra-
tion. A blind tied tongue,
equidistant from 2 scales
filled with grudges.

She is trying with all the powers of her mind to compel
Claire to call her on the telephone.

The wise Claire had been too wise to come flying with
her to the parents' 100-year-old stone house on the hill
in St. Helena. Despite their pledge to share all their
burdens all the time.

But then: she had not asked the wise Claire to come
flying into her past with her. & scar her wounds of
memory with the timeless wisdom of her presence. It
had not occurred to the visiting daughter that she
might be sitting alone between the parents. That she
might not be sitting across from her twin sister Laura.
Whose face is becoming a flame-haired mirage, at the
other long side of the dinner table. Peeking out from
behind the fresh white roses in the antique silver bowl.
—From which rises a subtle white perfume.

Laura's presence at the dinner table would instantly
break the deadlocked silence between the parents.
With more authority than blunt wisdom. With the
greater authority of her handicap.

Made still greater by having overcome it. By not allow-
ing it to stand in the way of a brilliant career. Laura
has founded an all-woman law firm, in Los Angeles,
which specializes in international marriage laws &
customs.

Which she is currently investigating, in Portugal, for a
book she is planning to write. Which she is planning to
call: *Women, Owning & Owned.*

She has not come home for Christmas, for the first
time since she left for Boston, over 12 years ago
—unlike the visiting   normal   daughter who has
come home for Christmas for the first time since she
left for New York   France/Denmark/Norway/Eng-
land/Gibraltar/Greece/France (again) /Italy/Spain/
Portugal   over 12 years ago.
because she is spending this Christmas in southern
Portugal, in the Algarve, sorting out her notes: As both
parents have been telling their other   visiting   daughter. Several times. On separate occasions. Whenever
one or the other parent leaves the room. Or gets out
of the car. Or goes upstairs to take a nap.

—With an identical ring of pride in their separate
voices.
Which sounds like an accentuation of her own lack of
achievement, to the visiting daughter.
Who is normal
& has no excuse
but dropped out of college 1/2 through her first year
(2 weeks after her visit to the college psychiatrist)
& drifted from country to country, allegedly studying
the techniques of the old masters. Questionably
financed by the occasional sale of a painting.
Or of her body.
Who is a drifter more than she is a painter, forever in
pursuit of questionable artistic/spiritual/or plain car-
nal quests...

At least that is how the visiting, normal daughter
thinks herself thought of by both parents, in juxtaposi-
tion to the pride she hears in their voices when they tell
her about the absent Laura.

Who would be telling about her experiences in Portugal, if she were sitting at the dinner table, in the place of her mirage. A frail, flame-framed Botticelli face, repainted by Vargas for a gas station calendar. Or by her namesake, their grandaunt Laura. Equidistant from either parent. Who would smile. & nod. & ask questions, at the expense of the silence between them. Questions which Laura would answer. Readily. Easily. Would have no reason not to answer. Because, for as long as the visiting, normal daughter can remember, her twin sister Laura has been saved from unanswerable questions by her handicap.

The visiting, normal daughter has also traveled in Portugal. For almost 1 year, exactly 1 year ago. But she can't tell the parents about her experiences, for fear of inviting their questions.

Separate questions, on separate occasions, but prompted by the same basic curiosity; or concern: How had she lived what had she lived on for almost 1 year, in Portugal?

If she tells them the truth: that she painted murals in exchange for her room & board —which would impress them; not as much as doctor-of-law Laura's investigation of local marriage customs impresses them...but still—

the father would want to know: How many murals she painted, & of what size, in exchange for what quality room & board? Did she have her own bathroom? (Yes, Dad, with a short, deep cork-plated tub...), in retrospective protection of her interests.

& the mother would ask for detailed descriptions of technique, medium, style, & subject matter, as a "minor" fellow artist, the niece, & granddaughter, &

great-great-great-granddaughter of "real" artists.
Pointed questions. Which the visiting, normal daughter would hear as implications of a lack of thorough-
ness on her part; of her facile superficiality & unde-
served rewards. She always feels like a sham, compared to the mother's preoccupation with perfection.

Since her arrival the evening before, she has felt that
the mother has been putting her under a microscope,
to check her culture.
—Even though the mother insists on referring to herself as "only" a fashion designer. Whose "modest
accomplishments" were, moreover, "snipped in the
bud" when she became a horseless, maidless housewife, & a mother   of twins   in America.
—The mother hasn't even had the opportunity of
being a has-been... Which may be one reason why
she's finding it so hard to get back into fashion designing. Which she has been trying to do lately, on the
"most modest of levels"...
—The mother is probably lucky to be designing ski
suits for children, at her age. The juvenile sportswear
manufacturer to whom their backyard neighbor Marcia Campbell   —who is a "real" painter—   was kind
enough to introduce her, probably thinks that she's in
her second childhood, & may therefore understand the
taste of kids...

_____Why does the mother seem to derive satisfaction
from putting herself down? the father asked the visiting, normal daughter that afternoon in his wine cellar.
Where they were picking out wine for their Christmas
dinner.   —Where the mother never sets foot: Wine
puts her to sleep. Even the smell of wine...
_____Why this mania of glorifying everybody else? the

father asked with a sigh. Her aunt/grandaunts/etc...
all of whom she considers "real" artists, compared to
her unaccomplished self...

——All of whom had had the same solid family
wealth to sit on, in front of their easels. They never had
to peddle their talents in the market place.

——A bunch of amateurs, the whole lot of them, in the
opinion of the father. Who enjoys the English meaning
of the word: "amateur." It amuses him to think that
English denies quality status to a "lover." His large
features look diabolical, with the stroke-slanted smile.

The visiting, normal daughter tries to remember if the
mother used to put herself down quite so much when
she & Laura were still living at home.   —When she
& Laura   had perhaps been too young/too self-absorbed to notice how the mother felt about herself.
About anything.
She can't believe that the mother really feels as unaccomplished as she claims to be, by comparison to their
backyard neighbor Marcia Campbell, for instance.
Whom she calls a "real" painter. Perhaps the mother is
putting herself down out of arrogance? Because she
feels so superior to everyone else   except to Laura
that she can't possibly live up to her self-expectations.
—While complimenting everyone else on his/her
peanuts. Which she considers "achievements", considering everyone else's inferiority...

Which the visiting, normal daughter didn't say to the
father in the wine cellar earlier that afternoon.
Which the father would have contradicted. Passion-
ately: He permits no one to criticize the mother.
Whom he has admired all his life.
—Who may *be* a genuinely superior person. Gen-

uinely modest; not arrogant at all..._____

In the wine cellar earlier that afternoon the visiting, normal daughter merely hoped that the mother would begin to feel better about herself, now that she had found an outlet for her sketches.

—A hope sincerely shared by the father; with a sigh: He feels very grateful to Marcia Campbell for giving the mother a break. That's why he bought the cat painting that's hanging in the upstairs bathroom...

The visiting, normal daughter had noticed the painting as soon as she arrived the evening before: A large metal disk   like a sewer cover   with seven pale grey cats walking from left to right, toward an eighth pale grey cat walking from right to left. The colors are pale grey & violet & match the mother's grey-&-violet-striped shower curtain.

She has also noticed a change in the mother's tone, when the mother speaks of Marcia Campbell. Compared to the mother's tone she thinks she remembers from before, from when she & Laura were still living at home. When the mother used to speak almost fondly of Marcia Campbell.

The mother sounds guarded now, when their back-yard neighbor's name is mentioned.

Which has prompted the visiting, normal daughter to ask herself: if the mother feels humiliated, sketching ski suits for children. If she suspects Marcia Camp-bell   —a painter who has been earning her living as a legal secretary—   of introducing her to a juvenile sportswear manufacturer to "put her in her place": as an elderly, comfortably supported housewife   —who has never had to balance her own checkbook—   who thinks she can make a comeback as an "artist"...

Or could the mother be imagining that Marcia Campbell has designs on the father, all of a sudden? That she
"seduced" the father into buying the painting from
her?

> The visiting, normal
> daughter frowns into her
> wine glass

at the thought that the mother   the parents   may not
have realized Marcia Campbell's sexual persuasion
during all the   30?   years she's been living in the
converted hothouse in back of them.
& at the realization that she has no idea how her
parents feel. About most things. About each other:
Does the father really disgust the mother, since he had
the stroke?
Does Laura know what they feel & think? Would
Laura really be telling them about her experiences in
Portugal   —openly; without self-censorship—   if
she were sitting in her traditional place at the other
long side of the dinner table, breaking the silence
between them?

Which the visiting, normal daughter would probably
intensify   directing their tacit condemnation of each
other also toward herself   if she started inviting &
answering their questions about her own experiences:

——Well, Dad: I was the only live-in woman in a 12-
cell monastery surrounded by cork oaks.
A one-time penal monastery, where heretical monks
used to be sent, to flog the dissension out of themselves. & each other. But now it has been converted
into an S & M retreat, by its new owner, who was
given the former monastery as a present for his 21st

birthday, by his mother, because he "preferred a monastery to a castle..."

Well yes, Dad, Mother: I was hanging out with the local landed gentry. The Portuguese branch of an international homosexual elite. On whose fringes I was being tolerated as a hired artist, as in the days of your Medici. I painted murals while visitors of all nationalities passed through the one-time monastery like so many heretical monks. Anglo-Saxons mainly, but also visitors from Spain & France.

—No Italians, though. At last not while I was there.—

They all knew the new owner. Or knew friends who knew him. He was famous. Notorious, I guess you'd call it. A striking-looking young Portuguese, with steel-blue eyes & dark curly hair.

A perfect model for the punishing archangel, Mother. A different punishment for each cell, but always the same punishing archangel.

12 murals, Dad. 8 × 10 feet.

12 different, differently punished monks in sexually suggestive poses of penitence, Mother. Each in the style of a different painter: Titian Velazquez Dali Chagall Renoir Rouault Evans et al. All heavily varnished.

& a 13th mural, Dad, 18 × 35 feet, for the communal dining room.

A "Last Supper," Mother. All diners but one portrayed as transvestites. Wearing satin sheaths, high-heeled pumps, & feather boas. & heavy make-up.

—Except for Judas, whom I portrayed as a sailor.—

I painted that one as a Manet.

You look shocked, Mother. Dad. But you are atheists, unlike me.

—Unlike most of my international models. & our Portuguese host. & his Portuguese mother, who'd occa-

sionally drop by & inspect my progress. & all their Portuguese live-in servants, & the servants' wax-faced children.—Sacrilege doesn't exist for you. Except in the form of social abuse. How can my paintings shock   or titillate   you? No one was being abused. All my models were consenting   titillated   adults.
Except, of course, the servants' children. Whose wanderings through the house at all hours of day & night might strike you as a sacrilege. As social abuse.
(Portuguese children never seem to go to bed. & they never seem to cry...)
But they were all well fed. & clean. I used a number of them as ornaments, framing my murals in the tradition of 14th-century illuminators.

—Did you know that quite a number of medieval illuminators used to be women, Mother? Anonymously painting under the collective signature of a father / brother / husband / master's workshop. Who didn't always sign their work either. —

Stocky, oval-eyed, wax-faced 6-8-year-olds, standing in doorways, pensive, with a finger in their mouths, looking into rooms where couples of men lay/stood/knelt/crouched in unusual contortions.
Boys and girls still too young to help with the daily chores, running   or tip-toeing   to their mother/father/a grandparent, to ask the meaning of what they had seen. & being told that what they had seen had no meaning. That it was peculiar to the behavior of the masters, & had nothing to do with real life...

—Although: the father or grandfather had, at one time or another during his adolescence, probably been "broken in" by his master. Who had, thereafter, cho-

sen his wife for him & godfathered the baptism of his
firstborn.

Who had, in turn, been broken in by the same master
…& so on & so forth, ad senilitatem…—

If Laura were here, she might tell you about some of
these well-preserved Portuguese feudal practices. As
sidelights of her investigation. If Laura's investigation
is permitting her to live close enough to the local customs to observe such sidelights. But I, your visiting,
normal daughter, cannot tell you about them. Not
without implicating my way of life, in Portugal.

At best I could quote the French sailor to you, my
Judas model, who liked to tease our steel-eyed, dark-
curled host, saying that: Europe stopped at the
Spanish border…

Which did not amuse our host.

& might not amuse you either. You might think that
I'm trying to put down Laura's trip.

When nothing is further from my mind. It was Laura,
after all, who cabled me the plane fare to New York,
after I called her collect in the middle of the Lisbon
night/in the middle of a Thursday afternoon in Los
Angeles, in her law office. 1 week before Christmas, 1
year ago.

I don't know your attitudes about abortions, Dad-
Mother. That's why I called Laura for plane fare. I
trusted Laura not to insist that I produce a niece or a
nephew for her   twin nieces or nephews perhaps
regardless of *my* needs. Or feelings. My fear of carrying Laura's deformity in my genes…

Yes, Mother: There seems to be an organic longing to
keep the child one feels inside. To let it ripen, & find its
shape. But in my case that would have been inconsid-

erate to the child. Not every woman has the talent to be a mother. I'm old enough to realize that my "creations" are meant to be in image only...

—Did *you* find fulfillment as a wife & mother, Mother? Wouldn't you be talking to Dad if you had? & break this unbearable silence. & not put yourself down quite so much... —

No, Dad: I'm not prejudiced against European doctors. —Or Portuguese doctors, if Europe stops with the Spanish border.—As a matter of fact it was a European doctor a French gynecologist named Claire Fontaine who performed my abortion, in New York City.
Where she has been performing abortions since long before they became legal.
Claire Fontaine happens to be the aunt & guru of my Judas, the French sailor from Toulouse. He sent me to his aunt in New York —at Laura's expense—
to make sure that I'd be treated like a patient. Not like a murderess, who deserves not to be given anaesthesia by an avenging patriarch, a righteous punisher of women who have "sex like a man." Women who walk away from the consequence like a man, instead of making a career of motherhood...

You're quite right, Dad-Mother: I might have taken precautions. But I hadn't anticipated getting pregnant, considering the monkish environment in which I was living. However, not all people are as immutably fixed in their sexual positions as the two of you at the opposing heads of your authentic grey-polished dinner table. I don't mean to imply that I set a gay man straight. I leave that illusion to the missionary types, who think

that the poor guy is gay only because he hasn't had his
chance with them. Or that a woman is gay because she
has never met a "real" man.

The French sailor & I weren't trying to reform each
other by making love.

& perhaps we weren't making love so much as friend-
ship. A touching of souls, which unexpectedly con-
densed into a life.

—Which took the risk of being curtailed when it chose
us for its parents...

The French sailor & his aunt believe   as many
Hindus believe; as I have also come to believe   that
we choose our parents.

Not always wisely, as perhaps in the case of your
aborted grandson / granddaughter / grand twins of
either sex, or one of each.

—Although: is it so wise to come into this life on the
eve of another Biblical disaster. Another holocaust, be
it man-or nature-made.

—What nonsense! you protest unanimously. Startled;
frowning in disgust at the broken silence between you.
At your continued agreement, as you proceed to tell
me that our borrowed Eastern belief is nothing but
rationalization. To ease our guilt feelings about the
abortion. To permit the French sailor's aunt to exer-
cise her profession. A sloppy moral convenience.

But think a step further, Dad-Mother. Don't you have
to agree also that it forces you to accept full responsibility for whatever you are. Whether you're beautiful,
or average, or handicapped, or talented. Or a mixed
breed. You certainly can't go on blaming your parents
for the kind of life you're leading...

I don't know how glad you are to see me, Dad-Mother, but it was the belief that I had chosen you for my parents that enabled me to fly out here this Christmas, to visit you for the first time in over 12 years.

Although, quite frankly, I don't think I'd have come if I'd known that Laura wasn't going to be here. I came out mainly to talk to Laura. To talk to Laura instead of listening to Laura, for the first time in her & my lifetime.

I wanted to tell her what the French sailor said to me. About both of us. After I told him that everybody who had screwed me during our adolescence had been in love with Laura. & had been chosen by Laura to screw me.

That Laura continued to rule my choice of lovers long after we'd begun to live apart. That my mind continued to don her copper hair & long grey eyes   & her hump, & her pathetic legs   every time I made love to someone.

_____Often out of a sense of obligation. Almost mechanically, as though I were a stand-in, distractedly performing through a screen.

—Hiding behind Laura's hump, for fear of exposing my own: the French sailor said to me.

I was just as irregular as Laura was: he said: but on the inside. Where no one could see it. I carried a hollowness inside me that was the concave mirror image of my twin sister's back.

—& harder to overcome, because I considered my invisible deformity unavowable, because I thought I had brought it upon myself. Whereas I thought that Laura's hump had been imposed by fate.

—Unless that was my doing also, if I thought I had

perhaps stolen my twin sister's food, & kicked her around inside your womb, Mother.

—Which used to haunt me, sometimes, during our adolescence. Especially when Laura was in pain...

It was arrogant of me to think that I'd had all the choices, & that Laura had had none: he said. Laura's otherness was her doing as much as mine was mine. Laura's soul had chosen the hunched back & the breakable legs as a conscious handicap in this life, to be exempted from temptations of the flesh.

—Which my soul had taken upon itself: I had chosen the appeasement of other people's lust. Without desire on my part. Or love. Or warmth. Or pleasure even. Which my soul had preferred, for fear of physical discomfort. A coward's choice, which was why I was ashamed of it.

My invisible handicap needed as much love & compassion as Laura's visible one. But it was ashamed to reveal its need, for fear of being seen...

I needed love. & Laura needed sex: he said to me...

You'll probably question the validity of a sailor's notions in matters of psychology, Dad-Mother. But talking with him helped me a lot more than the talk I had with the psychiatrist, before I dropped out of college.

—Yes, Dad-Mother: I'd been sent to see a psychiatrist, by the dean, the third week after my first Christmas break.   —For which I didn't come home. Most of which I spent in the Metropolitan Museum in New York.

Please don't ask me why the dean sent me to see a psychiatrist. It really wasn't important. All about a drawing I'd made of a girl with horse teeth. & it wasn't the reason why I dropped out. I felt I wasn't learning

anything. At least not what I felt I needed to learn to
become a painter.

Or for dealing with life. Which used to weigh on me
much of the time, ever since I became aware that I
existed.

—You don't know, Dad-Mother even Laura doesn't
know that I tried to commit suicide a couple of
weeks after our 12th birthday. Laura was back in the
hospital for something a stomach virus, I think, &
the three of us were sitting at this dinner table in a
dank-flannel kind of silence not so unlike the one
we're sitting in right now.

—Which makes me wonder if you two talked to each
other then. Or if maybe Laura & I always did the
talking during meals mainly Laura & that I never
noticed.

—That first night that Laura was away at the hospital
& I had our room all to myself, I stuffed my mouth full
of kleenex & pinched my nostrils shut until I blacked
out.

When I came to, I was in a panic. Gagging, vomiting
paper mâché mixed with dinner all over myself. I no
longer thought of killing myself, I felt too sick. I continued vomiting in the bathroom for maybe an hour.
As noiselessly as I could: I didn't want you to come to
the door, Mother, & ask if I was trying to imitate
Laura, so I could be with her in the hospital.

You asked me that anyway, the next morning, when I
wouldn't eat breakfast, & probably looked like hell. I
didn't answer & you didn't insist when I marched off
to school.

"When the disciple is ready, the teaching appears":
says the French sailor. Quoting his aunt, who is his
guru.

Who has also become my guru.

I obviously wasn't ready to hear what the psychiatrist had to say to me. Perhaps I needed the added dimension of faith: "All that is visible must grow beyond itself, extend into the realm of the invisible. Thereby it receives its true consecration & clarity & takes firm root in the cosmic order..."

You probably think that I'm a hypocrite. Or under the spell of one.

For whom you'll have downright contempt when I tell you that it was the French sailor's idea to portray Judas as a sailor, on my big Last Supper mural in the monastery's communal dining room. To portray Judas as the only "male." Which excited everybody & earned me many compliments. Even from our steel-eyed host, who normally reserved the male roles for himself.

Everybody liked the "otherness" of Judas.

—Whom the French sailor doesn't see as the tradi-tional traitor. He thinks that Judas' kiss was the seal-ing of a pact. A link via the flesh beyond the flesh, that enabled Christ to make himself visible to his disciples, after his death.

We sealed a similar pact to release the image of Laura from my mind when he kissed me. Under a cork oak. In the shadow of the moon.

For the first time I was able to feel myself alone inside my skin while making love.

No, Mother: I have not taken leave of my senses. On the contrary.

No, Dad: The French sailor was not the first "real" man in my life. I told you: He's gay. Remember.

But he definitely was my first real friend. The first

person who let me talk about myself. Who listened. While he posed for me.

We had become very open with each other by the time I finished the mural. Warm & relaxed. Perhaps because I was the only woman in the monastery, & therefore neither a sex object nor competition for him. I don't know. Maybe because he could speak French with me...

You're surprised that I learned to speak French, while drifting through the museums & churches of France, Dad-Mother? I also learned to speak passable Danish/ Norwegian/Greek/Spanish/& Portuguese. —Besides the more than passable Italian you took such pains to teach Laura & me, Mother.

I don't know about Laura, but I pick up whatever language people speak around me. That's part of being a sponge...

Don't deny me the satisfaction of a little self-depreciation, Mother. Even if my being a sponge depreciates my early training in linguistic awareness. By a linguistically aware mother...

Who insisted that her daughters speak the pure Tuscan Italian of Dante, at home. & learn to keep the two languages cleanly separate in their infant heads. & grow up to be truly bilingual, instead of acquiring the father's fantasy English. Which is grammatically correct, but sounds like a comedian telling Italian jokes: What's a Wopsickle? An Italian on a stick...

Which has never ceased to make the mother squirm. & may have contributed to the father's success as an undertaker. The father still says: "iz shoes" for issues, & "mal fatta" for: as a matter of fact...

A thing badly done?

Our host celebrated the finished dining room mural with a party. After an elaborate meal

—that began with a typical Portuguese fish soup, Mother. (Maybe Laura ate it too, somewhere in a restaurant. & copied the recipe for you, being your more thoughtful daughter. I'd warn you to go easy on the salt, though: Portuguese soups all tasted over-salted to me...) & great quantities of *vinho verde*, & the most delicious sour cheries in brandy after dinner—

a procession of pensive, bare-assed monks in brown burlap robes circled a high-flaming fire in the center of the inner patio. Holding open leather-bound volumes with blank pages in their hands.

I had been leaning against one of the columns on the periphery, thoughtlessly staring into the flames, when I had a vision of our dark-curled archangelic host, impaled on a thick pole, with sparks sizzling from his steel-blue eyes & perfect teeth.
The vision was so real, I felt someone ought to warn him. Perhaps the ghosts of heretic monks weren't taking kindly to his parody of their penitence. Someone he'd listen to. Someone with more authority than that of a feudal artist, who was, moreover, of the unauthorized sex.
The French sailor from Toulouse was sitting cross-legged on a narrow bridge that leads from the inner patio to a low-walled vegetable garden. I went over to him. He got up as though he had been waiting for me. It was a full-moon evening. We climbed over the low wall of the vegetable garden & wandered about for a while among the surrounding cork oaks. Which had

just been stripped, & were still bleeding through their cheesecloth wrappings.

Eventually we sat down on the protruding roots of one of them.

Making love was like the natural conclusion of our many talks. Warm & fluid. An underwater dream ritual.

Incidentally, my vision has since come true: Last September our host drove his Maserati into a lightpost at the edge of a small North-African airport, & electrocuted himself. The news arrived in a letter from the French sailor. It was glued so tightly that opening it gave me the strangest sensation of his saliva congealed into rubber cement.

—The letter was addressed to his aunt & me. Because I'm living with the French sailor's aunt in new York, Dad-Mother.

—In a Spanish-speaking neighborhood known as the *Loisada* (Lower East Side in Spanish pronunciation.) Where twin girls are called "twinas," not by their proper Spanish name: *gemelas*.

Where the gynecologist Claire Fontaine owns a 2-storey white brick building that used to be a synagogue. Now it has a doctor's office on the ground-floor, filled with Spanish voices. & a tiny backyard. & a female Saint Bernard named: Dr. Beast.

—Where I feel more at home than I remember feeling anywhere before. More than here, in your authentic 100-year-old stone house, in your authentic landscape, where I was born.

Where I never felt at home. Not even before I left, when I didn't notice whether or not the two of you were speaking to each other across this dinner table.

Not even upstairs, in Laura's & my twin-bed room.
When Laura & I read each other to sleep with Mon-
taigne.
When I dreaded being separated from Laura. Even for
one night.
I've always felt like your "other" daughter, Mother...

> The visiting, normal
> daughter has not found
> the magic word to break
> the silence between the
> parents. She has been eat-
> ing more than she nor-
> mally eats   more than
> she should eat   for want
> of something to say. She
> has cleaned out the sec-
> ond   small   bowl of
> Spanish cream, at the urg-
> ing of the father, & is
> lighting a cigarette.
> —Does Laura still
> smoke? she asks. In a vain
> attempt at conversation.
> The mother sighs: Yes. &
> leaves the table & the
> room before the father
> can start telling how hard
> it was for him to quit
> after he had his stroke.
> Picking up a habit was a
> lot easier than dropping
> one. His life has been feel-
> ing like a long slow wean-
> ing process: he says.

Of course Laura
shouldn't be smoking
either, with her lungs
compressed by her defor-
mity: he says. But then,
why deprive her of every-
thing. After all, all of life
was fatal...
He is smoking one of the
visiting, normal
daughter's cigarettes
when the mother returns.
Carrying 3 antique gold
cups of espresso on an
antique white porcelain
tray.
The father stubs out the
cigarette.

Which makes him feel embarrassed. Doubly embarrassed: in front of his wife for having no will power. &
in front of his   visiting, normal   daughter, for acting
like a guilty schoolboy in front of his wife.

—Caricaturing the supportive, trustworthy father
image   financially supportive & emotionally trustworthy   which he has been trying to project, since the
arrival last night of this other   normal   daughter.

—Who has been on his mind a great deal, during the
past 12 years or more. More so than his   deformed;
formidable   daughter. Laura. In whose shadow she
grew up.
For which he has been blaming himself, for the last 12
years or more. For not knowing how to show his sup-

port   during the girls' adolescence   how to tell his
"other" daughter to enjoy her normal healthy body,
without seeming to stress Laura's deformity.

Blaming himself when he found out   —from a post-
card from Copenhagen, 4 months after the fact—
that his normal daughter had dropped out of college.
& begun her restless drift from country to country.
When she didn't come home once, in over 12 years.
He has been wondering about her reason for having
come this time. If she has   or needs   a reason. Other
than being closer to home again, back in the U.S. In
New York, where she seems to be living now.
On what?
Where she seems to have been living for about 1 year.
Which seems a long time for her to be staying in one
place.
She was just as close to home last Christmas, when she
didn't come...
He would like to think   but can't   that it is filial con-
cern that has brought her back to him. But she can't
have known about his stroke. Nobody can have writ-
ten to her about it. She'd never given an address, on the
over 12 years of postcards they'd received from her.
About a dozen or so postcards a year.
—Unless she'd stayed in touch with laura. Perhaps
Laura had received letters from her normal   still
overshadowed   twin. Detailed reports of her twin's
erratic existence. About which he knows nothing.
Which Laura keeps secret...although Laura never
seems to keep secrets. Never seems to have any secrets
to keep; from anyone...out of a tacit twin-sister sol-
idarity that excludes the rest of the world.
Even their parents.

Especially their parents. Who made their normal daughter feel that she had no home to return to, after she left for college. & dropped out. After her separation from Laura, whose shadow had been the only home she'd known.

Because the parents' attention had always been riveted on their deformed daughter. & couldn't be deflected onto their normal daughter, who felt that their interest in her would be strained by anything that went beyond a casual hello on an address-less postcard.

Unusual postcards, with jaunty captions, from places she had probably left by the time they'd receive her cards.

Which he had collected. In the right top drawer of his desk in the downstairs study. Always leaving the last card out, standing propped against the pencil sharpener on the window sill, until the next one arrived.

He has followed her seemingly directionless course, traveling with her in his mind. Trailing her on maps from a Norwegian fjeld (Norway, the "Latin" country of the North) to vineyards along the Rhône (You were right, Mother, red wine does stain the teeth) to a Greek temple on Sicily   (Empedocles slept here). To a cluster of bandaged cork oaks   (Are cork oaks male or female?)   in southern Portugal.

—Where his formidable daughter is spending Christmas this year.

Which may be the explanation for his normal daughter's unexpected visit. She may have come in Laura's stead, if his daughters have stayed in touch behind their parents' backs.

—At least behind the back of their father.

Perhaps Laura had sent her sister the fare, forcing her to come in her stead, to keep their parents from choking on the silence between them, at their Christmas dinner table.

Where neither parent would have felt free to read through the occasion. Unlike through ordinary everyday meals, through which the mother has begun to study fashion magazines & sketching manuals.

If Laura is concerned with   if she's even aware of the silence between them. & wanted to give her itinerant twin a taste of what she   Laura   has sat through, for well over a decade of Christmas dinners.

Through which Laura had never seemed to stop talking. Unlike her twin, his visiting, normal daughter. Who doesn't seem to know what to say. To either of them.

Who may of course have come home mainly to see Laura, with whom she may not have stayed in touch any more than with her father...

He knows nothing about the life of his visiting, normal daughter. Yet, he still feels closer to her than he has ever felt to Laura. Even though he has been seeing Laura 6 to 8 times a year, & has always known where Laura lives   (He has been to her apartment in L.A.; as has Laura's mother).   & on what   (He has also been to Laura's office.).   He knows   & admires   how Laura earns her living.

Which he would also like to know about his visiting, normal daughter. But so far he hasn't found the opportunity to ask her how she supports herself...
Painting?...   He doesn't want her to hear his question as criticism. On the contrary: He wants her to feel

that he respects her way of life. & that she can count on him in case of need.

Ever since her arrival the evening before he has been toying with a thought. A proposal he wants to make to her: That they go traveling together. To places she has as yet not seen. & can't possibly afford to see on her own. How would she like to go to China with him, for instance?

He had meant to lead up to his proposal earlier that afternoon, when they'd been alone together in the wine cellar. He, too, has always been a traveler at heart, he'd meant to say to her. Even their coming to America that first time had filled him with excitement, despite their reason for leaving.
Unlike the mother. Who hadn't wanted to leave. She still hasn't made peace with her American life.
Who was finding his presence offensive, since he had the stroke. Which was making life uncomfortable for both of them in their comfortable house. Her mother barely spoke to him, as she must have noticed. Etc. & so it might be a good idea if he gave her mother a vacation from his presence. & went traveling.
Which he could afford now, at long last, in his retirement. & how would his daughter like to go traveling with him. To places she had as yet not seen... Etc... To China... Etc...
Where he used to dream of going when he was his daughter's age. When he'd been intrigued by Chinese medicine...

Anticipating her enthusiastic gasp. But she had responded with caution to the first mention of her

mother, & they had ended up discussing Marcia
Campbell's painting in their upstairs bathroom.
Which he understands. He doesn't expect his visiting,
normal daughter to take sides, during the short time
she is spending with them. 1 short week. Laura has
never taken sides either. Although her mother's treat-
ment of him can hardly have escaped Laura during her
many visits.
Even a person as self-absorbed as their backyard
neighbor Marcia Campbell seems to have become
aware of it lately.
& it visibly isn't escaping his silent, visiting, normal
daughter right here & now at the dinner table.
—Which makes him wonder if both his daughters
have perhaps been hearing lies about him from their
mother.

He had called his visiting, normal daughter into his
downstairs study, for a glass of wine before dinner. To
lead up to his China proposal once more, by showing
her that he had collected all her postcards, in 4 neat
rows in the right top drawer of his desk. & surprise her
with his detailed knowledge of all the places she'd
been to. But when he opened the drawer to show her,
the postcards had disappeared, & a stack of unused
old tax forms was lying in their place.
Which had upset him too much to say anything. He'd
barely been able to raise his glass to his visiting, normal daughter. Who had raised her glass; with a faint
smile. & they had sat across from each other, sipping
& faintly smiling in silence.
She would probably not believe him now, if he told her
that he had collected all her postcards. She'd probably
think that he'd thrown them out, after a cursory
glance, & a frown about her instability. Perhaps a

begrudging chuckle over some of her funnier captions.
—Only the last postcard she'd sent   from New Jersey
early .that summer   was still standing in its usual
place on the window sill, propped against his pencil
sharpener. A painful photograph of a wild Canada
goose, its neck caught in a plastic 6-pack holder.
—Which she probably thinks he kept out of sadism,
because he enjoys the sight of suffering, as an ex-doctor turned undertaker. If she believes her mother's
insinuations, making him out to be a monster while
he'd earned everybody's living.

His speech had sounded noticeably slurrier   at least
to him   when he'd finally broken their silence &
asked her about the postcard.
Which had been made from a photograph, taken in
her presence by a friend who had a summer house on
the Jersey shore: she'd told him.

—The friend had spent 11 days stalking & trying to
feed the wild goose.   _____Which she had painted
from this & several other photographs. The creature
had been too frantic for her to sketch it directly. It had
been under constant attack from other wild geese, that
kept swooping down, hacking at it every time it tried
to eat.
Eventually her friend had caught it, & managed to cut
the plastic 6-pack holder   —in which it had trapped
itself, diving for food—   away from its neck, at the
risk of being gashed by its frantic beak. Her friend had
finally managed to free the bird, with infinite patience.

Which has made him think that his visiting, normal
daughter may not be living alone, in New York. That
she may be painting at the Jersey shore in the summer,

& in the city in the winter, supported by the patient
goose-saving friend.
& that she may, therefore, not be interested in traveling with her old father. To China, or anywhere. That
she is, at present, traveled out. & wants to stay with
her friend. At most she might be willing to put up with
a visit from her old father, in New York or at the
Jersey shore...

The visiting, normal daughter feels the father's eyes on
her. Scanning her normal   average   profile. The blu-
ing trail of smoke issuing from her average mouth &
nostrils as she lights another cigarette.
She wonders how the father would have reacted, in his
downstairs study before dinner, if she had told him
that her friend at the seashore is a woman. The French
gynecologist Claire Fontaine, who performed her
abortion.
Who is allowed to practice in the U.S., where the
father was not allowed to practice, when he arrived
from Italy.
How would the father feel if he knew that she has been
living with that woman, Claire Fontaine, happily for
exactly 1 year...

She has no idea what the father thinks about "wom-
en's women": as Laura used to call the guests that
came to Marcia Campbell's Halloween parties.
On which she & Laura used to spy, during their
adolescence. When the wall-size usually brightly lit
windows of the converted hot house were hung with
black velvet, & Marcia's cats could no longer go in or
out as they pleased.
She & Laura had once locked themselves in the upstairs bathroom   ostensibly washing their hair   &

watched Marcia's guests arrive.

The beanstalk lady in a blue tuxedo, with silver hair, alighting from an open silver jaguar

the stately "twins" in pink & pale-blue bunny suits, heaving themselves out of a beige station wagon

the leather woman, encased in shiny black from head to toe, on stiletto heels, with several pounds of thin gold chains around neck & waist, swinging herself over the handlebars of her motorcycle...

Watching them disappear through Marcia's black-draped door.

Does the father know & not care about Marcia Campbell & her friends. Or has he never noticed them. Or has he noticed them, but thought they had come costumed for Halloween...

———As the mother had, perhaps. Until recently. Until Marcia Campbell introduced her to the juvenile sportswear manufacturer. When Marcia Campbell had perhaps given the mother to understand that she expected something in return. Something more tangible than the mother's consistent praise of Marcia's "real" art, compared to the mother's own negligible attempts.

& was that why the mother sounded guarded now, whenever Marcia Campbell's name was mentioned. Because the mother had enjoyed Marcia Campbell's tacit, never-threatening courtship. & was outraged now by the sudden breach of hypocrisy. Seeing immorality, suddenly, where she'd seen nothing but originality or quaintness before.

Unless the mother has allowed herself to be seduced by Marcia Campbell? Or has perhaps had a secret relationship of long standing with Marcia Campbell,

which had perhaps come to an abrupt end when the
father bought the cat painting. Prompting guilt feelings in Marcia, but not in the mother.
All of which seems most unlikely to the visiting, normal (?) daughter. Despite the realization that she cannot gauge the mother's reactions to most things.
—She may even be imagining the mother's guarded
tone.

She wonders if the father is as opposed to abortion as
she knows the mother is. As she discovered that morning   shortly past noon   in the kitchen. Where she'd
found the mother working on their Christmas dinner
when she'd come downstairs. Still in her nightgown.

The mother keeps a radio in the kitchen, permanently
tuned to a 24-hour news station. She stirs/chops/
cracks eggs to a background of muttered news. On
which she occasionally comments to anyone who
comes into her kitchen. Anyone except, of course, the
father.

The mother had stopped her electric egg beater to lis-
ten to a flat male voice announce the suspension of
welfare-funded abortions. Which she acknowledged
with a grim nod.
Turning the radio up, for the benefit of her daughter.
Who had been slouching against the sink, drinking
left-over breakfast coffee, & consuming cigarettes.
Who had misinterpreted the mother's nod, & said: I
knew it. That's the first step. Soon it'll be illegal again.
Which the mother had hoped that it would be. Grimly.
—I certainly hope so: she had said.
Shocking her daughter out of the caution with which

she has been listening to everything both parents have said since her arrival the evening before.

You can't mean that, Mother! An independent thinker like you. You can't be agreeing with people who want to deny women the right of decision over their own bodies!

MOTHER: It's because I think independently that I refuse to subscribe to legalized murder, in the name of liberation & equality.

DAUGHTER: You don't think women are entitled to the same sexual freedom men have?

MOTHER: The way I hear you say freedom sounds like license to me. & I don't think that women   *or* men have the license to play around with life.

DAUGHTER: Do you think that men   who can't get pregnant   should be allowed to force women to stay pregnant against their wish. Priests   the Pope   who aren't even supposed to know about sex...I always thought you were an atheist...

MOTHER: I don't need to believe in a god to object to legalized murder...

DAUGHTER: What about the other legalized murders, when these compulsory babies become soldiers...
—Which is probably what they're being "saved" for in the first place.

MOTHER: That's different. Then they can decide for themselves. Now they can't.

DAUGHTER: Even if that were true   even if 18-year-olds *could* decide if they did or didn't want to kill   don't you think a grown woman should also be allowed to decide how she wishes to use her body.

MOTHER: It seems to me that she made that decision when she got herself pregnant.

DAUGHTER: Did you *decide* to become pregnant when you did, Mother, with Laura & me?

She had regretted her question as soon as it came out. Thinking that the mother must hear it as a reference to Laura's deformity, which they'd been discussing earlier. As an inference of blame.

But the mother had suspended her hearing. The father had entered the kitchen in quest of lunch. He stood, refrigerator door in hand, looking questioningly from the mother's instantly turned back to his normal, visiting daughter slouched against the sink.
—To whom he said: Good morning...

_____Which she had *not* heard as the criticism the mother affirmed he had intended   —It was after all past noon. Well past 3 P.M. in New York; did she always get up so late? —   after the father had walked out again, carrying his luncheon tray to the porch.

Do the parents agree on public issues, while living in perpetual private disagreement?
Which she may be imagining: How can they disagree when they don't speak to each other...

Perhaps they think the way they think because they were born in a Catholic country. That was turning fascist during their adolescence.
Perhaps their childhood & adolescence had been the happiest years of their lives   —at least in retrospect, seen from beyond an ocean & a continent—   & they were echoing opinions they had heard with happy ears. Which nostalgia forbade them to question.

—Despite the hardships these opinions had caused them. They knew from personal experience that independent minds & Jews were the historical targets of

Catholic & fascist crusaders, yet they refused to see
any connection between the inquisition/concentra-
tion camps/& the uncivil liberties taken with the lives
of women.
Treating women's bodies as collective property, over
which the individual owner has no say…

She wonders if her own opinions are also childhood
echoes. If they are Californian opinions, from Napa
Valley; from St. Helena. Still, after over 12 years of
absence. Although she had been anything but a happy
child.
Although she had become aware of her unhappiness
mainly afterwards, after she'd left St. Helena & lived
away from Laura. Despite the attempted suicide.

& Laura's opinions?
Would she & Laura still agree about most things, if
they were facing each other once again across the
parental dinner table, after leading almost contradictory lives for over 12 years?
Would they still know exactly what the other was
thinking, & confirm it with a blink, or a pursed
mouth. A hand to the forehead, one of Laura's favorite
gestures: Lord have mercy…

Would that have been the 31-year-old Laura's reaction —hand to forehead— to the French sailor's
suggestion that Laura needed sex…
About which she'd planned to talk with Laura. To talk
with Laura had been her main reason for flying home.
Home: another mechanical childhood echo…

What would Laura have said to the mother in the
kitchen that morning?

That they were experiencing a generation gap. That
the mother was no longer of childbearing age, & could
therefore afford to dismiss the problem of unwant-
ed   unaffordable   pregnancies with a man's detach-
ment. A man's dynastic indignation.

Was the mother hoping to avenge her wasted talents
which she felt she had sacrificed to motherhood   by
forcing younger women to live in similar frustration.
Like the arthritic Chinese empress who decreed the
custom of bound feet for her court ladies, to make
them as crippled as she was.

Forcing generations of "well-born" Chinese women
to hobble, in order to be socially acceptable...

Which Laura could have afforded to say to the mother
in the kitchen, with the impunity of her handicap.

—Which didn't exactly mark Laura out for child-bearing either. In spite of the French sailor's recommenda-
tion. & might therefore incline her to share the
mother's views.

—Which the mother had affirmed Laura shared.
Absolutely!

—Which Laura couldn't be sharing, or she wouldn't
have cabled her the money to fly from Lisbon to New
York to have an abortion. 1 year & 1 day ago: last
Christmas eve.

When she had fallen in love with Claire.

She is lying on a stirrupped table inside a white brick
cube, that used to be a synagogue & is now the office
& residence of the gynecologist Claire Fontaine.

—Whose name means: Limpid Source...

A reddish light   magenta mixed with flesh; which
turns out to be a Lower East Side winter sunset   is

tapping her eyelids. She blinks through a gauze of
tears, & finds herself staring up at the same short,
blunt-curving nose & finely arched eyebrows above
China-blue eyes she had stared at in Portugal, painting
Judas as a French sailor into the 18 × 35 foot diningroom mural at the monastery.
The face above her is older; topped by a crow's cap of
greying hair. An older Judas, & who is a woman.

Claire had taken her hand & told her not to mistake
her tears for guilt. That most women wept copi-
ously even after normal deliveries of healthy, wanted babies. That tears were the female body's common
reaction to being unoccupied again. A relief as much
as a loss.
In a soothing voice, full of love. With the same clarion
of rolled r's that had always made her smile during her
talks with the French sailor.
& brought back just such a feeling of relief mixed
with loss which had swept through her after she'd
finished his portrait. & the mural.
& the memory of other rare occasions, when she
had finished a painting, & felt pleased with it. &
sorry disoriented that it was finished. When she
had also been close to tears.

Claire's voice had brought other tears of insane jealousy to her eyes later, every time she heard her soothe
other patients in that same loving tone —especially
in French, soothing a Haitian patient— after she
started working with Claire. Choking on swallowed
screams of: Me me me ONLY ME!

Which she'd never thought of screaming at any of

Laura's capriciously selected lovers. Or at subsequent lovers she'd picked up on her own   with Laura in mind   after their college separation.

Or at the French sailor.

Least of all at the French sailor. Who looked so much like his Aunt Claire. Except for longer, as yet not greying hair hanging into his eyes.

Who had exorcised the witness of Laura from her sex life.

Me me me me me me me. The mechanical mindlessness of jealousy had turned her into a robot. That gave appointments. & checked   mostly Spanish   names. All the while keeping a painful record of every loving word & gesture Claire wasted on the unworthy.

On ballooning women of all ages with wax-faced children attached to a trailing hand, that filled the waiting room with odors of yellow lard & fried bananas & belched-up milk. & sometimes spilled over into the small backyard, pester-petting the saintly Saint Bernard.

A robot that confused love with sex. & sex with exclusive ownership. & neither heard nor saw the Claire on whom she spied. Whose indiscriminate kindness made her suffer as only a robot can suffer.

—& take refuge in guilt: to explain away the robot's responsibility for being so miserable. Explaining her pain-discovered heart as her punishment for the expulsion of Laura. For excluding the thought of Laura from thoughts of Claire. & unrequited sex.

—For having deprived Laura of vicarious childbirth, when she aborted Laura's potential niece.

—Since Claire had told her the sex of the fetus.

Whom she   & Claire   had saved from being "caged

in matter": if she believed Claire. Who believed that
"procreation was the cruellest act, because it forced a
spirit to become a body."

Which had struck the hurting, fault-ferreting robot as
a convenient belief, for a gynecologist who performed
abortions.

It would certainly be the parents' unanimous verdict,
if she started telling them about Claire & her beliefs.
—Without breaking the dinner silence between them.
Each parent would wait to be alone with her to express
the same negative opinion about her "employer."
...In whose house she shouldn't be living. Couldn't
she find some other job...
& they would continue to disapprove of Claire on
every separate occasion for the remainder of her visit.
Catching up with over 12 years of disapproval of her
wayward life. Their pent-up worrying —which was
perhaps the parental form of love.
...Urging her not to fly back to New York. To stay put
for a while, & look for a job close to "home"...
Which both parents might urge her to do, out of the
same separate desperation disguised as worry-love:
To have someone to talk to, in their 100-year-old
mausoleum on the hill.

Where the visiting, normal daughter doesn't think she
can last the week she had planned to stay.
She has been thinking: Call me, Claire...call me...
call me...through much of the Christmas dinner.
Chewing her Christmas food in the rhythm of a silent
incantation.
If her thought messages don't get through, she'll try to
sneak out to the phone booth outside the all-night

grocery store at the foot of the hill sometime after dinner, & call Claire.

—Who neither lies nor takes oaths, & may be reluctant to call her back at the parents' house with a professional pretext for her immediate return, unless she can convince Claire that the emergency is real, as far as her sanity is concerned.

The parents won't dare disbelieve a professional pretext, because of their atheist belief in the sacrosanct priority of work... If their visiting, normal daughter has a job one that can't get done without her she must be leading a normal life, in New York City.

Unless their continued silence at the dinner table drives her crazy enough to start babbling to them about Claire.

I'm living with this fabulous woman doctor from Toulouse, Dad-Mother. Her name is Claire Fontaine. That's her real name, & that's exactly what she is: A clear fountain...

You needn't raise both your eyebrows, Mother, just because I live with a woman. I work with her, too. I've been working with her for almost 1 year, every day until yesterday, when I left her for the first time since I met her, to fly out here to see you...

—To see Laura; to talk with Laura: since Claire's beliefs are teaching me not to lie.

—Perhaps not even to save my sanity...

Claire is not like your backyard neighbor Marcia Campbell, Mother. Whose name has been producing the same alienated expression on your face. An expression I don't remember from before I left. At least not in connection with Marcia Campbell. Who used to be

your favorite neighbor; unless I misremember: 12
years is a long time.

How long have you known that Marcia Campbell is
gay? Or don't you know? —Either of you? Because
you're too set in your positions to conceive of any
other?

But then, why that same alienated look when I tell you
that I'm living with a woman, Mother? Do you really
feel so bad about yourself that you've begun to dislike
professional women! But you like Laura...

You used to like your aunt...

Perhaps I was equally inflexible when I assumed that
Claire was gay   that she was like her nephew who
had sent me to her   when I first met her.

When I fell miserably in love with her.

& felt rejectd by her 24 hours a day, watching her
"love" her ugly patients.

For 2 pain-programmed months I walked around like
a robot. The robot-twin of a deformed, angel-faced
human being who was the keeper of our single soul.
Hating Claire for treating me with the infuriating
kindness of serenity.

Until my robot-self finally came to realize   to my still-
smarting shame   that, in Claire's case, the philosophy
had preceded   even prompted   the choice of her profession.

That Claire Fontaine was one of the "purified." A
"perfected" "good woman." An anachronous fol-
lower of the Cathari.

—Whose martyred beliefs the late-20th-century
gynecologist is trying to reapply, 7½ centuries later, in
her clinic that used to be a synagogue on Manhattan's
Lower East Side. The Spanish Loisada...

As is her nephew, my Judas, the visiting French sailor
from Toulouse   as yet somewhat less serenely   in
southern Portugal
— Where Laura is spending this Christmas, sorting her
notes. —
in a one-time penal monastery.
Whose original inhabitants had perhaps been sent to
their punishment for holding similar beliefs.
For being followers of Mani, the 3rd-century Persian
monk who fused the teachings of Zoroaster, gnostic
Christians, & the Buddha into a single message of
peace.
Which may have felt closer to the true teachings of
Christ, to those Portuguese monks, than the king-
making/king-breaking precepts of Rome. Which may
have struck the monks as being diametrically opposed
to everything Christ had taught. & lived.
... As though a (the) devil had destroyed Christ's
work, substituting a false church for the true...: as
was the firm belief
— the heresy —   of the Manicheans
the Arians
the Bogomiles
the Paulicians
the Priscillians
the Albigensians
the Cathari   — a name which historians
                    either derive from Greek, meaning
                    "purified" (as in catharsis), or from
                    the German word *Ketzer*, meaning
                    "heretic"... depending on the his-
                    torian's childhood-molded perspec-
                    tive of history...
the Waldensians...

A cosmopolitan list of sects. All accused of heresy, like the Portuguese monks in their 12-celled as-yet-mural-less penal monastery.

The 3rd-century Persian monk's message of peace & tolerance set off a millennium of persecutions. By popes & kings. By crusaders sincerely convinced that they were marching on the one-way road to God.
By indebted landowners whose property could not be touched as long as they were away on their sacred murder mission.
—By saints: It was Saint Dominic who invented the inquisition. The admired friend of the gentle Saint Francis, whom he embraces in a kinship of faith.
But also the friend of Simon de Montfort, one of the fiercest exterminators of my friend Claire's Cathari philosophy... Until his death, in Toulouse, on June 25, 1218, "by a mangonel operated by an unknown woman"...

Which had made me laugh when I first passed through Toulouse. Long before I met Claire. Even though I didn't know what exactly a mangonel was. Nor that I was laughing at the death of my future friend's most hated person in the history of her city. An "enlightened" fanatic who had gouged out the eyes of over 100 Cathari prisoners, & cut off their lips & their noses, to make them look like faces of death, before sending them on to the next Cathari stronghold—led by one whom he had spared 1 eye—to create panic among its defenders.

From the 3rd through the 13th century, herds of men & women were intermittently

decapitated
driven into moats & crushed to death with boulders
burned alive

> — with their books: leaving no trace of
> the positive side of Cathari teachings
> (except for "supra-substantial" instead
> of "daily" bread in the Lord's Prayer);
> only the biased records of their
> inquisitors —

> — sometimes inside their houses. With
> their pigeons, their messengers of
> peace, that stayed around the burn-
> ing roofs, scorching their wings until
> they fell burning or burnt to the ground —

for the salvation of their heretical souls.

Unless they fled, carrying their harried beliefs from
3rd-century Persia to Bulgaria to Spain to Portugal to
northern Italy to Germany to southern France.
To 11th-century Toulouse.
Which experienced an age of enlightenment, under the
administration of Cathari "good men"   as they were
called by grateful contemporaries, whom they taught/
nursed/... "consoled," on their deathbeds.
They were also known as "the Weavers," because they
often used weavers' shops to do their teaching. Until it
became too dangerous for them to assemble at all,
even underground.

You probably know more about these long-haired,
dark blue-robed vegetarians
—who'd let themselves be killed rather than kill
even an animal. Whose prolonged meditations & fasts

gave them the pale telltale complexions that later
denounced them to Saint Dominic's inquisitors—
than I did, Dad-Mother, until I met Claire. From your
history classes. Where both of you learned "twice the
stuff" they were teaching Laura & me at our St.
Helena high-school. As both of you kept telling us.
Where Laura & I were learning American history...

Of course you know about them, Dad:
Their religious tolerance attracted many Jews to the
French south. Doctors & savants who shared their
interest in herbs, anatomy, & the stars.
& you too know all about them, Mother:
They were trend setters in the arts.
They attracted the first troubadours, with their social
tolerance, their democratic disregard for hierarchy...
But did your better Italian schools also teach you that
Dante initially planned to write The Divine Comedy in
occitan? The *langue d'oc*, the *provençal* of the early
troubadours?...If he had, you couldn't be quite so
proud of your pure Tuscan, Mother.

My friend Claire learned about the Cathari before she
learned to read or write. From still existing traces of
them in & around her native Toulouse.
Before she studied their official history in her   also
European: also better?   school. & became converted
to their way of life by many contradictory books she
continued to read about them. In which they're called
"tardy pagans," or "the forerunners of the French revolution," or "the first original free thinkers"...

Who encouraged not only religious tolerance &
democracy, but also sexual equality. At least by implication, since their faith denied the "reality" of the

sexes by denying the reality of sex. Of life in the flesh.
Whereas the Church of Rome was staunchly anti-
feminist in practice.
Even though there existed as yet no culture gap
between men & women. Which was not introduced
until some 300 years later   during the 16th century
by parish schools that taught the boys, while the girls
stayed ignorant. Up to then, wives often were better
educated than their husbands, especially in the French
south during the Cathari years, when women enjoyed
far greater liberties than their northern sisters.
They held salons   like Esclarmonde de Foix, a digni-
fied elderly widow who had become a Cathari "per-
fecta"   & discussed religion & poetry with Catholic
clergy, Cathari "good men," & troubadours.
—Which so enraged a certain Brother Stephen of
Minia   a "foreigner & a boor"   who could not tol-
erate the sight of wisdom dressed as a woman, that
he told his hostess to "go tend your distaff, Madam,
it is no business of yours to discuss matters such as
these"...

_____But then, the gynecologist Claire Fontaine had a
number of similar experiences, over 7 centuries later,
when she first worked in New York as a physician
with the United Nations. To the consternation &
embarrassment of male patients from all 5 working
nations, & a number of others, who either refused to
undress, or else "flattered" her with an erection...

The Cathari implication of sexual equality made
Toulouse look like "Sodom & Gomorrah" to Simon
de Montfort   —which he vowed to destroy, in the
service of God—   even though this implication was
based on continence.

Parenthood   excuse me, Dad-Mother   was almost
as serious a crime as murder to the Cathari. They
believed   as Claire does   that conception degraded a
spirit by forcing it into the matter-sheath of a child.

That was not born with a soul, but had to work at
acquiring one, every moment of a lifetime made of
faith, hope, patience, & charity...

The "perfected ones" among them avoided all gratifi-
cation of the senses, including marriage. They always
lived with a companion of their own sex   —a
"socius" or a "socia"—   as a protection against the
selfishness of solitude. & the temptation of procreation.

—Which prompted the usual speculations that halo
the private lives of monks/nuns/sailors/prison in-
mates. Feminists.

—It prompts them still: as shamefully demonstrated
by my own initial robot reactions.

There are court records of accused heretics
—whom St. Dominic's inquisitors obliged to wear a
yellow cross sewn to their backs; or "2 crosses of a
different color than their garment," one to be worn in
front, the other in back... —

pleading innocent of heresy because they "were married"...

I wish I'd had your background in European history,
Dad-Mother, when I passed through Claire's Toulouse. That I'd known where to look for the odd-
shaped Cathari cross, which can still be found in some
obscure niche of some obscure church. Apparently.

Claire had a small silver copy made of it, which she
wears over her heart. It's very interesting looking.
Would you like me to draw it for you?

Don't bother getting up for a piece of paper, Dad. I'll draw it right here on the marble. I always carry a magic marker...

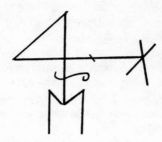

Don't worry about your table, Dad-Mother. I'm sure it'll wash off... with a little wine...
Unless you'd rather leave it for a while, to study it after I fly home to New York. Sometime tomorrow, probably, after I get the emergency call I'm expecting.

Please don't resent my calling Claire Fontaine my home, Dad. Mother. After all, it was she who urged me to visit you this Christmas.
Besides: I might never have fallen under her Cathari spell if I hadn't been born   & raised by you two right here in your stone-silent house.
... If we feel the way we feel & think the way we think due to the geographical coincidence of our birth...
As you led me to believe in the kitchen this morning, Mother, when you argued against legal abortion...
Which I can explain only by your having been born & raised in Florence, Italy. A city with a proud past of solid merchant wealth. Of which you had your share.

& therefore perhaps attached to "conservative" memories: thinking of children as "assets"...

_____Are there children who are assets to their parents?
Emotionally as well as "socially"?
Who talk to their parents about what really matters to them?
& parents who talk to their grown children about their true feelings. & concerns. About them. Or about themselves. If they know their true feelings about them. *Or* themselves. Their passing moods...

Perhaps Claire Fontaine could not have taken me in, into her synagogue-clinic on the Lower East Side, & nursed a pain-programmed robot into a "socia," with the infuriating patience of serenity, if she had not been born & raised in Toulouse.
A city older than Rome.
Through which I may have passed solely in preparation for meeting Claire in New York. To be able to situate Claire in the geography that molded her thoughts. In her historical past that supplied her with role models like Esclarmonde de Foix. Or the nameless operator of the mangonel.

Although Claire does not approve of killing, no matter what the justification. Cathari may commit suicide by starvation   a practice known as the "endura," which was tolerated, but not encouraged   & they must do their best to prevent life, but they may not take a life, once it is in existence.

Still, when she taught me the song her city sang in its

liberated streets after the death of Simon de Montfort,
her eyes danced with the words:

> Montfort es mort
> es mort
> es mort
> es mort
> Viva Tolosa
> Ciotat gloriosa
> et poderosa...

Would you like me to sing it for you, Dad-Mother?
To the tune of a Christmas carol, so you can sing
along. I don't think I can go on listening to your silence
another minute...

The visiting, normal daugher is trying to fit the words
of Claire's city's song to the tune of The Little
Drummer Boy, in her head, when

> the phone rings in the liv-
> ing room.
> She flies toward it, with
> the teenage reflex that
> used to send her flying to
> answer Laura's lovers'
> calls.
> But the bushy voice at the
> other end belongs to
> Marcia Campbell, who
> says: "Hi Laura"... &
> asks to speak to either
> parent... if they're not
> too busy to come to the
> phone...
> The parents are looking
> expectantly at the visit-

ing, normal daughter
when she returns to the
living room. Before she
informs them that their
backyard neighbor is on
the phone   ... for either
of them...   Before she
slides back into her seat
& resumes her slouched
position.

The mother looks at the
father, arching 1 eye-
brow.

The father reaches for his
glass & takes a long swal-
low of wine, preparing to
say something.

He doesn't get to say it.
The mother has risen, &
disappears into the living
room.

The father clears his
throat. His speech
offends her, he says
again, shaking his head.
He'd had a hunch that
this was Laura calling: he
says: Funny, when he
knows that Laura is too
far away...in southern
Portugal...

Before he asks: If the visiting, normal daughter is
expecting a phone call?
From New York? with a

smile that invites   &
offers   complicity. She's
not: she lies: No...not at
all...
Just a teenage reaction,
probably, sitting once
again in her old place at
the parental dinner table...
He nods. Smiles. He's
glad she's come home: he
says...

...Although...

The visiting, normal daughter has a change of mind.
Thinking of the phone call she plans to make later that
evening. & of the emergency call she hopes Claire will
make, that is to allow her to fly back HOME to New
York...

...it's always possible
that I get called back to
New York: she says: I
work in a hospital. Peo-
ple always seem to get
sicker during the holidays...
The word hospital has
caught the father's attention, & quickly, before he
can ask her any questions,
she asks him if he knows
what a mangonel is.
Or was.

Which the father knows.
Balestra: he says trium-
phantly in Italian.
Catapulta: he says:
Onager...   giant war
engines that used to deal
out the most terrible
slaughter... during the
middle ages... hurling
stones... sometimes dead
bodies... they used to call
them "Her Majesty" or
"the nasty neighbor"...
He laughs. He is beam-
ing. Brimming with unex-
pected knowledge.
He is telling the visiting,
normal daughter that the
guillotine was invented
by a French doctor, a
humanist who had seen
too many botched necks,
when the mother returns.
She stands, leaning
against the frame of the
dining room door, look-
ing from the father to the
daughter to the father.
Her left eyebrow arches
almost into the roots of
her still thick, still bluish-
black hair.

She is hardly surprised to hear an ex-doctor turned

undertaker talk about death machines. With glowing
enthusiasm.
He probably dreams of using them on her, but can't
accommodate his public image with outright murder.
Like Amyas Paulet, Mary Stuart's last jailer.
Like the barber who accused his wife of aristocratic
connections, during the French revolution...
Mediocre men, forever plotting the annihilation of
women they can't dominate...

> Marcia Campbell is invit-
> ing them over for eggnog...:
> the mother says into
> the silence that has fol-
> lowed her reappearance
> at the door. She pronoun-
> ces: eggg...noggggg...
> with a grimace.
> Why don't you two go:
> she says: she thinks she'll
> stay & do the dishes...
> & maybe get a little more
> work done on her kiddy
> sketches...
> The father protests: She
> doesn't want to offend
> their backyard neighbor
> ...who introduced her to
> the juvenile...
> O, but *he* bought one of
> Marcia Campbell's cat
> paintings. Their back-
> yard neighbor will be
> much gladder to see a
> patron of her art than a

Johnny-come-lately in
need of being patronized...
The visiting, normal
daughter looks fixedly at
the mother, braced
against the door frame of
the dining room.

Blocking her planned way out. How will she get to the
phone booth at the foot of the hill if she can't get out of
going over to Marcia Campbell's with the father.
—Who will think that she, too, is offended by his
speech, if she refuses to go with him. But if she goes, it
may be midnight before they get back. 3 A.M. in New
York. Way too late to call Claire, who opens her clinic
at 8 every morning.

Marcia Campbell isn't
interested in seeing her:
she says. Looking fixedly
at the mother: Marcia
Campbell doesn't even
know she's here. She
called her Laura on the
phone...

Which has started to ring
again, in the living room.
This time, the visiting,
normal daughter does
not jump up.

She can feel the father looking at her, smiling a slanted
accomplice smile.
She doesn't want to confirm his insinuation that she's

waiting for a call from a New York lover, & spoil her
irrefutable professional alibi.
Besides

>   the mother is closer to the
>   phone. & has already
>   gone to answer it.

...& is probably telling Marcia Campbell that her
husband & her   other   daughter will be right over
...in case this is Marcia Campbell once again, to say
that she meant to include "Laura" in her invitation...

Nothing warns the visiting, normal daughter that this
might be Claire. On whose voice in her left ear she had
concentrated all during dinner. Underlying all other
thoughts, until the call from Marcia Campbell.
She has no hunch. No foreboding. She is genuinely
surprised when

>   the mother returns. &
>   says: For you... In a flat
>   tone, belied by inquisi-
>   tively arched eyebrows.

>   The visiting, normal
>   daughter stays on the
>   phone for a very long
>   time. & without speak-
>   ing, it seems. At least so
>   far as the parents are able
>   to tell, as they strain to
>   listen from the dining
>   room. Separately
>   speculating about the
>   same indiscretions.

When she finally reap-
pears in the dining room,
her face looks so drawn
& grey that the mother
reaches for her
daughter's elbow, &
makes her sit down. In
Laura's chair

                    of all places.
Obviously they have no foreboding either.

They're leaning into her
face from their respective
sides; sacrificing the
silence between them to
their unanimous determi-
nation to make her stay
the full week she'd told
them she'd be staying.
—After all, they haven't
seen her in over 12 years.—
   To wait until the
next morning, at least,
when it would be easier
to drive her to the airport.
In daylight. Both parents
insist on driving her to
the airport, in the morn-
ing, when she tells them
that she must leave at
once. Tonight...
Never mind, she'll call a
cab...

She doesn't mean to sound impatient with the parents,
but she has to get away from them, out of this house,
before she screams at them that Laura is dead.
—Which Claire just told her on the phone…

Unless it slips out of her in a whisper. & she sits
trapped between them, on Laura's dining room chair,
whispering answers to their questions.
Her voice muffled by the same stunned disbelief that is
amplifying the parents' voices: They are loudly de-
manding to fly with her to New York. To Claire's
synagogue-clinic. & charge Claire with murder.

With the double murder: of their daughter Laura & of
their potential grandchild. Their potential granddaughter, since Laura had also been pregnant with a
girl.

To whom Laura couldn't have given birth even if she
had wanted to. Because of the deformity compressing
Laura's organs.

—She wasn't cut out to be a child-bearing mammal:
Laura had said to Claire before the abortion. With an
angel smile. Which Laura had continued to smile
through the abortion, until she died. Clutching
Claire's left hand   so hard she'd broken Claire's left
middle finger…

A triple murder, including the first one, committed
exactly 1 year ago, on the same stirrupped table: of
another, earlier granddaughter, not born to them by
their other   normal   daugher. Whose normal organs
could easily have born them a grandchild, but who
had decided to wash it out in a flood of tears.

But whose normal mind was not able to wash out the shock of Laura's disappearance from her life. Of no longer having or being a twin, as she sits staring wordlessly into the parents' bowl of white roses.

Whose subtle white perfume may be an emanation of Laura's soul.
Unless they'd had only one soul between them. & she has now grabbed it all for herself: fulfilling the old Italian woman's warning of 30 years ago. Which the mother had repeated to her in the kitchen earlier that morning.
Perhaps she had denied Laura her due of their shared soul when she stopped sharing her sex life with the thought of Laura. After making love with the French sailor. Her model Judas. Claire's nephew.

Who had perhaps offered Laura the sex he'd said Laura needed. If he had somehow met Laura while she was sorting her notes in southern Portugal. By the strangest of coincidences.
—Which crosses her mind, stunned with disbelief.

_____She has as yet not seen the ledger Laura gave to Claire to give to her, in case she didn't survive the abortion.
Detailed records of every lover she can   or cannot remember. Including a xerox copy of her drawing that had upset the roommate with the horse teeth. Since the day she & Laura separated to go to different colleges, over 12 years ago.

She does as yet not know that Laura had her trailed: from New York to France to Denmark to Norway to England to Gibraltar to Greece to Italy to France

again: Toulouse   to Spain. By waiters/concierges/
grocers/teachers/professional detectives.

Until Laura decided to trail her herself   at a distance
of 12 months   to the penal monastery in southern
Portugal...

There are copies of the letters Laura wrote to all the
remembered   & not-remembered   — suddenly re-
remembered —   lovers. In a style that is a modern
adaptation of the style of Ninon de Lanclos.
—Whose definitive biography by Emile Magne Laura
also gave to Claire. To give to her, in case she didn't
survive the abortion.
& the originals of the replies from those lovers who
apparently enjoyed writing letters.
& transcripts of telephone conversations Laura had
had with those who didn't.
& an 8 × 10 color photograph of her portrait of the
French sailor. Taken without the context of her 18 ×
35 foot dining room mural.
The tangible evidence of which has as yet not caused
her to hide her eyes in her hands, as she sits on the pew-
like bench in Claire's waiting room.

> She's still sitting in
> Laura's place at the par-
> ents' highly polished grey
> marble dining table.
> Between the standing
> parents, who are anx-
> iously leaning in on her
> from their respective
> sides.
> She does not look at

them. Or speak to them.
She is staring straight
ahead, into the bowl of
white roses, wondering if
Laura knew she was liv-
ing with Claire. If Laura
had asked Claire to send
her away   to St. Helena
to the parents   to be alone
with Claire for her abortion.
If Laura would have tried
to take Claire away from
her, if she had lived.

The father has drawn
back the drapes to check
the weather for their
drive to the airport.
There's a reddish moon
outside, & on an impulse
the mother switches off
the light.
After a gasp of darkness
reddish pools start glis-
tening on the marble sur-
face of the dining table.
They look like wounds to
the staring visiting, normal daughter. Glistening
scabs of memory, at
which the mother
scratches with arthritic
shadow fingers, as she
gathers their glasses &
cups.

Pamela Zoline
Busy About the Tree of Life

'**Brilliant and original, Pam Zoline is a wholly new voice.
Her vivid, witty and highly intelligent prose is a joy to
read. "Heat Death of the Universe" is one of the
greatest short stories of the past 25 years**' – J. G. Ballard

From the meditative complexity of 'The Holland of the Mind' to
the pastoral pastiche of 'Sheep'; from the bizarre and unnerving
biographical history of 'Busy About the Tree of Life' to the
classic science fiction story 'The Heat Death of the Universe',
Pamela Zoline proves expert at transcending the limits of form.
The interwoven themes of all the stories – of love, death and the
imagination – are explored within a complex narrative
framework that constantly challenges accepted notions of
writing and reading.

Subtly humorous and intellectually rewarding, these are stories
to read and re-read.

Fiction/Short Stories   £3.95
ISBN: 0 7043 3998 6

Maria Marcone
A Woman and her Family

Franco – a born patriarch, intent on turning his children into two perfect, well trained puppets

Marta – sixteen, fiery and volatile

Marco – fourteen and a half, 'a child without defences'

Maria – forty-five, a teacher, torn between her rôles of housemaid, cook, wife, mother and analyst of the family . . .

When Marco falls seriously ill, and Marta becomes so anorexic that they fear for her life, Maria is forced to examine the family system in which they are all embroiled.

An intense and thoroughly involving story that will haunt you long after you have finished reading.

Winner of the Villa San Giovanni Prize, 1977

Fiction   £3.95
ISBN: 0 7043 4056 9
Hardcover: £8.95
ISBN: 0 7043 5031 9